# Geometricized

# Historico-

# Mysticism

Like a recovered pyramid text in which all the ancient myths we thought we understood have been recast, Evan Isoline's *DΣVDMVTH* is a disorienting phantasmagoria of genre-shattering forms and styles, tearing like blitzkrieg through its unhinged imagination of the unconscious space behind all time. Spastic, batty, unrelenting, absurd, provocative, incantatory, and profane on every page, consider making this the last gift you ever give the people you call your parents...

**—BLAKE BUTLER**, author of *Alice Knott*

In Evan Isoline's *DΣVDMVTH*, words walk like zombies called forth by the dead end of infinity. The text (r)evolves through multiple fonts and forms, every page transpierced with visionary transgressions akin to those of Lautréamont or Lovecraft. *DΣVDMVTH* depicts the cold heat of a *vanitas* for this post-historic era, "a grammatical plea / written in pi."

**—ANDREW JORON**, author of *OO*

Evan Isoline's *DΣVDMVTH* moves at the pace of a mystic's pendulum — a swirling, hypnotic oscillation, an "unfurling twilight in the place of meaning." This "neo-gothic" work is saturated in the hypnagogic plane of "deserted orbs," "lunar bouquets," and "tombstones shaped like hearts." Isoline evokes the surreal philosophy and slant spiritualism of Jean Genet in the compulsive trance of *DΣVDMVTH*. Like all occult texts, this book has probably found you for a reason. Get mesmerized.

**—CANDICE WUEHLE**, author of *Monarch*

Evan Isoline's new book is both geometric and sprawling, both impossible narrative and prophesy, but most of all its a work of visionary protest.

**—JOHANNES GÖRANSSON**, author of *Poetry Against All*

*DΣVDMVTH* reads like a ghostly erotic call from beyond. A call for revolution. A text that rebels within itself, a text that reads the writer. Language like fingers slicing through air and pulling out the guts of an imagination that the average day has worked so hard to train us to not see. *DΣVDMVTH* is Isoline's highest achievement yet. A book full of magick that speaks directly to the stars.

**—THOMAS MOORE**, author of *Forever*

# DƐVDMVTH

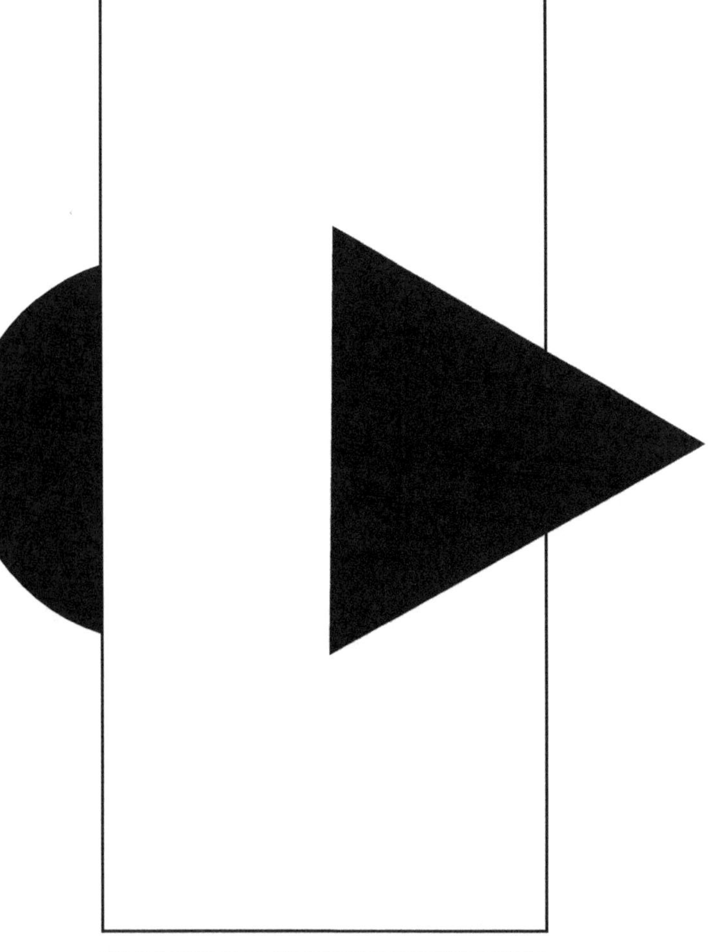

**EVAN ISOLINE**

# contents


Yours, Deadboy

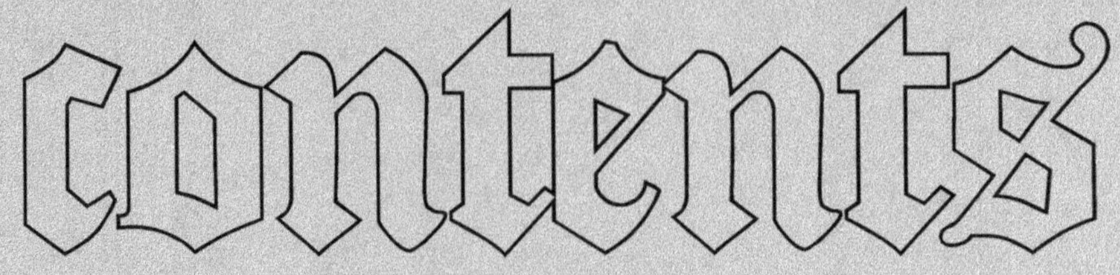

"Salivation On All Meanings, For All Occasions" :
De Propaganda Fide Novi Spiritus Sancti I.

Abscissa of Thistles

The Dusk of New Venus

Red Air

DEADMATH

Piss All Suns

Gravestone Blister

The Celibate King

Cosmophobicon Halla

Et Tu Antechamber

Dear History,

I play the role of the jester in saying in the name of intelligence that it definitively refuses to formulate anything whatsoever; that it lets loose not only the one who speaks but the one who thinks.

**Georges Bataille,** *Inner Experience*

The Hermits Prayer & the Widows tear
Alone can free the World from fear
For a Tear is an Intellectual Thing
And a Sigh is the Sword of an Angel King
And the bitter groan of the Martyrs woe
Is an Arrow from the Almighties Bow
The hand of Vengeance found the Bed
To which the Purple Tyrant fled
The iron hand crush'd the Tyrants head
And became a Tyrant in his stead

**William Blake,** *The Grey Monk*

There is no religious denomination in which the misuse of metaphysical expressions has been responsible for so much sin as it has in mathematics.

**Ludwig Wittgenstein,** *Culture and Value*

*For Cassandra*

yours,

deadboy

Here we wait, for the vessel of history to open, and,
winter in your eyes, to set thaw upon the cheeks of
my glowing idyllic embodiment, mutating, grotesque,
into even nastier future-regimes of social crucifixion
that I, day by rabid day, sculpt away, so that you
can alight upon my unimaginable evening of beauty.

At last it is here, eleventh hour, eleventh winter,
eleventh self, stripped of all disguise, gracefully
purged, spontaneously lovely, sweetly resolved.
This, the grim will of the Enlightenment, is my
story. An epic of fools, told for the delight of
fools. I wryly turn time into an apology of lies,
a self-justification, longing to believe that for
the poet, sympathy, finally, is an unnatural emotion,
concocted by an invention of the self. Such are
the agonizing and frightening truths that I repeat
over the following myth, to wit, of whether the
mathematical valedictory mood arises naturally upon
a single individual, or, on the contrary, depends
on the relative density of the crowd he finds
himself among.

In my awful designs, I will pervert the forms of
communication, and the formulas of reality, so that
when I pour into you the delights of my dispassionate
temperament, you shall partake my rapture and come
away outraged with my indignation. For here and now
my exasperation is incalculable or, ad infinitum,
unsentimental and free of all pretense of judgment
and the treachery of self-love. Thus alone do my rude
and brutal muses clothe my limbs with verme, and my
underlinen with flowers and garters of my own stink.

––––––––––––––––––––––––––

Proof is a condition of demonstration, desperation, and conciliation. My love of order is fear of chaos. At the threshold of comprehension, reason and protest, anarchy and proper dialectics, I offer you my sickness. But you are on your merry way, and reason has crossed this threshold long ago. And where reason flees there is madness. Thus I say to you: where everything is in progress, madness has already arrived. I have seen the future, and I can't go back.

Lovers of chaos, woo me to my wedded bliss. Let the lovers of disorder woo, for they shall be called the lovers of paradise. Seduce them to me under starry disquietude, because I am on my way to a palace of order. My dear disquietude, come into paradise, so that, within the new order, madness may find its haven. Arguing, I lie to you, and apologising, I lie to myself.

Will the snow eat our sweetness as we grow numb to our solace? Will we fade into soft pastures of unknowing such that our disdain towards illusion is erotically satisfying? Woe betide that poor vessel if it reveals the bloom to the walking dead. We of the revolution are co-dependent subjects exposed to a human hoax and for what? Your future within my ending. I trust you will find me worth the trip. We restitute each, secure in the hour of our mutual extremities, the apex of an absolute and impotent utopia.

Oh, Guerilla, how I've missed you. Tall and fair. You are the fruit of the hope, the seed of the revolution. I'll see you soon, and I'll tell you why I kiss you with burning lips, somewhere so perfect and secluded. Here, we come to the page, to the white page of winter.

Ignorance is suicide, so is knowledge. We are torpid as to our fate, we are cast upon the passion of our raptures, as I am cast upon you, a salamander with eyes of granite, seduced by the lure of an inviting and byzantine idleness. I will assume a gesture that involves you, paradoxically me, an offering to the great emptiness within us both, yet say not a word, for your curious paste of fury is my sagging pearl compassion. Your lamb's cheek is my pilferage with stupendous erosions, and at last I shall weep, to make of the dead the happiest of audiences.

You are the applauding amanuensis and me as if my tongue were a silvery conference of suns. Taste and mood lift as if tastes and moods were weights. Molt me, hurt me, I have nothing to counter the revolt, when romance tilts me from that beacon, that incantation summoning a belief in my heart.

What is the smallest unit of belief, in this realm where all time is malign?  Here I enter the second stage of self-recognition, where I assume a ludicrous, hopeless and impotent bravado, in a decision you undertake as if the idea of being dead was life-giving.

I respond obscenely, to a bizarre enquiry into my potentialities, my divinity with no clear high-ground, my bestiality taking the flavor from the molecule in the juice of fire.

I play a fool and smile a smile as some cold thing of guts runs down the narrow ugliness of my laughter, no authority to grant me climax until you evaporate, until the Goddess of Day has put out my eyes.

Then, in the morning, you have no choice but to cut yourself loose in my loathing. And so the story of my misanthropy will set out, step by step in the manner of a zoology of manners. Who knows from what waters I may jerk off into the wild azaleas, flinging at the air from the vanity of my arrogant kingdom, that great unbending bow of indignation like one of the high sentinels of the sky?

I am cast onto this passion by sadistic chance, and I am neither right nor wrong. It's all language, I'm drowned in it. I struggle against the desire to delay the terminations of this sentence. Who can begin to hope what is to come on the morrow of this braying? And if at dawn I rise and behold you as I write this, then, all quite different and rendered in still more odious colors, we will begin the tragic poetry of my psyche.

The vessel of my revenge will not be a pink satin wardrobe filled with giggling girls, gaily passing in their large dresses down some creaking corridor. It will be a recondite torture chamber, stern and netherly capacious.

Where there is room for the perceptive judicious torture of belief toward which your movements reflected, it is, no doubt, so for all the puppetmasters and all the pantomime prisoners of this gorgeous letdown, to end upon the cone of white diamond snows of the pale sleep. As a test, I contrived on a chessboard to read your mind and the nervous flaccid fingers of your control over me. Shame on me for such impure materiality, for at last at that point we would be pure and immaculate and purposeful, in the forge of eternal absolutism.

What else could resist the full spell of the enigmatic grandeur of my undying, my incandescent, leaden sentence-shell of sarcasm? It will be my ugliest weapon against all the fabrications of your plain little lives.

The lacerating beauty of my vengeance, the etymologies and allegories of my malicious historical present. I will confound your alibis with the gesturing imbecilities of slavish futures and sluggishly clinging pieties. I will take you for what you are, and that you will no longer be perceived as someone or something, but as a cipher. Be unveiled then, exposed as to the realization of pure nihilism, of apparitions that I was and would become, and my vulgar mood has dissipated like your hellenistic sweat, I am naked, as the Roman umbrage was naked in its sight of the process of decay from glory to doom. In the bottomless boredom of my indifference I will let you dress me then in the debris of your peculiar shams and hypocrisies, your laws and your mores, your inherent aesthetic vices and your unalterable virtues. I will spill your categorized shibboleths about the English language. I will infuse a spirit of defiance into your aeons of pedantic, pontificating elan.

Because mathematics is the poetry of the apathetic. The first lesson of mathematics is the principle of Infinity. The second, which is the lesson of finitude, tells us that the concept of what can never be is identical with what never was and never will be, namely an infinite number of things that are not. The third lesson is the true meaning of nothingness.

That one thing and another equal three and not two, is what my beset instinct contrives. My mathematics is the mathematics of sex, the mathematics of murder, with its accompanying vast unrealities of poetic ecstasy. In the intoxication of my mathematics, I'll appropriate your unassignable ideologies. I will confer your crowns upon your favorite absurd dogmas. I will dredge your creeds into quicksand, I will tempt your established systems, sweep away your conventions. I will leave no corner of your distinctive opinions untouched. I will push your notions to the farthest ends of the earth.

There are countless forms of me that I shall reanimate,
to which I shall lay claim in every circumstance of your
forays in time, of your worldliness, of your solitude,
of your eccentric individualism — what beauty, what
sorrow. I will confront your barbarities on their own
ground, face to face. I will inflict upon you the ugliest
vengeance that human anger can bring. Your tongue will
be sick with my geography. The mathematics of rage will
be the geometry of my ecstasy.

I'll bequeath my body to you, contemptuously spewing
forth its specialized exhaust, so that you may stand
on high, before other statues of mean contours like
gods in their starlight. Little poor vessel of history,
cast into my wildflower sluice all your paragonic
symphonies, blindfolded I will turn more patience
into a torn mask of a harebell, snuffling madly with
electrocution in its horrible tresses, with conundrum
and crime, oozing violet, as you go across the tormented
plateaus, looking back and seeing no one there, also
looking infinitesimally forward and finding nothing,
— and mouthing no words — the future having no better
claim upon you than the past. Both are empty.

Love and death, spring eternal as the diving of doves
in the air, thrive in what I have here conveyed to you,
like the fluttered petticoats of a boy king, my
fallen hero, your sanctity with gentle awe humbles
me. Start where there is a question or a beginning and
strive from there in identification to find a
solution. The knowing priest who murders time out of
self-interest because time is murder, and, the
scientist who is miserable to live when he can only
wish he had made a discovery as unexpected as time.
Dear useless stick insect, screw your slithery instinct
that shoots spitballs of gore behind your vile
yellow eyes, beetlestarred rich coward, screaming
at me "Why, Oh Why", beside an Aegean sea,
in small caves like Grecian towns between the
fissured rosettes of my eyeless mask.
A dung incubus is not a name that has ever been
mentioned in goodness.

I know it is a stretch but here we meet, my one hero to the end, deathfields till we meet again and beside you I felt that you could have loved — I never felt you could leave — there is no mirror we could make when the star dangles lifeless in this impossible encounter of love and death. No one will know who you are and thus you will be capricious and stealthily pretty. My will turns even the abrasions of your pelt into seams of violet moss, for beauty comes for whom it pleases, and grief is beauty's guest. The Paris of my smoke and Constantinople of my ink now bend to my sultry will, which is nature's will, and its consummation, leaving you to the decrepit, tiresome hours and the residue of being me, radiant before the expanse of my perfect grief... like a rose now opening, now emitting a perfume whose scent pleads — calls to memory.

It's funny, I've forgotten the meaning of history, but its whisper still greets me in the morning, all of the children are still there — their parents too — they are all alive, their arms raised and fingers parted into perfect V's in the school yard, each one holding a mirror to the sky.

I remember, I am like an old war film, and the scenery is littered with mirror shards. I hope the other actors like my makeup yet, undeniably, I am beautiful. You cast my whisper to the air and the beam of the world, your pout is like the sulks of a perverse hyena who didn't need a pièce de résistance so he installed a castle in your mouth. You know the language you speak is not our language. Not yet, anyway.

I too am haunted by my own reenactments. I wish it were a time of nothingness but one can't undo a time. I wonder which movies you watched, your false eyelashes thick with lanolin. They're certainly not my kind of movies. I do not want to speak of my love anymore, so we'll pretend this is not love, and say it's chemistry — but what do we know about chemistry?

As time passes, the sparkling blue starfish of your lips shall start to brown in the palms of my hands, my kisses will be as gentle as rain, but gentle rains cannot change the course of rivers.

I knew, it was best for us to be enemies, winter nights spent in movies, you who are riddled with visible bullet holes having wet dreams of Xibalba, crosseyed, dead as boys and girls who refuse to be otherwise. Dead as worlds that shouldn't be dead. Here's to the impossible dreams of the damned, old movies who bore us with their foreplay, here we are stuck inside the screen, blind as bats to love.

But I do not hate you, nor can I truly love you, your deadboy who cannot love and whose eyes flower in the night, the boy from the cinema, reminiscent, ascending towards the moist recesses of a supreme Pythagorica, poor darling forgive my disgust, and my rosary of peacock tears flissing irregularly in the brilliance of my solitude, and am I ever in a mood to be put on trial, for demasking the false father, the false king, the false queen who will never say my name — to kiss the weeping angel.

Here's to the angel, who never wants to weep, the star of everlasting youth, whose silver hair I long to touch, the dead are coming back and with a new kind of love for death, the show is sold out now the theater is cold and the audience too and oh, it's a winter garden, and I'm a princess in your heart, I'll be the queen of the princes' court, the black tulip queen of the night, who carries her dead lover's weeping head over the hills like a yellow sun.

You're blushing, mignonette, I've enflamed you so scorch me, in your blossom's breath-green fire, and thou in my arms violet, violet me, the effulgent spatial gloss of each projection, frilled without exception in white puce, fire-purple of the stained cathedral of Apollo, my eyes moisten with all the green angels in the bloom, the filthy stench of eternity's court, free of all but the most decrepit lover's wail in a crumbling rose garden.

Oh yes, there was my objective and it was a romantic love, My cowardice was well-placed but I might have been driven to it. Life conspires in the play of discontinuous sublimity, in that web of relentless outbursts in meantime of inexorable routines. Now forgive me for the one thing I've done. I've loved you, I've always loved you, even when I hated you. We all had to follow our roles. Life can be burdensome enough and yet even worse is that awful ambivalence which I've been stricken with.

Impetuous soldier, rosy soldier, I love you. Drift with me across the rooftops, primal wishes drip down like drops of static with the dawn, you said you would never forget the nadir, and I said I have forgotten the nadir ... but that I will never forget you. I'll drown myself in your indigo eyes, facing the bayonets of the militia.

To cut oneself through the broken glyph of history is to seek the myth of violence, the myth of death. Death is thus not death, may not be an end. The end of language is a beginning. Does its geometry not approximate that to which I am contrained?

Death is crystalline.

I did not mean to speak of my love but the shot of a wild rainbow refracting in the spring glass of your eyes... and the laughter of day you inspired... your cheeks painted pink, while mine bled cold... glossed with the golden sheen of a fresh Etruscan clay ...

My cloak, my sword, my rabbit ears ... together, soon the blue wolves would converge on your forgotten town, those silver eyes squinting in the sunrise of the summers, somewhere, a lone home burns, embers hissing, where the silence is worse than war: where a tyrant broods... history was there then.

To the East, the new sun is a weapon. I have put on my armor, I have painted my horse for war.

Come, follow me along a shimmer of barbwired avenues pressed, lush with end-arches, great elasmines of heather til dashed, we enter but a ridge of my endless, red-turned chrysoence dusted with pale mauves and verdure, the glowing vanilla constellation of teeming crystal placenta, painless and floating, an etiolated softness has settled in, constantly flaring the tulip laces of my harelip against the swollen gate, a delicately little woman in maiden's cap, lemon blades that bend the protagonist through polymetastasis, my eyelids inside of pink robin-red tearcups, inside my eyelids the diaphanous head of a beech, like a cherub's head, I weep against your face — soft, wet vanilla pollen.

Constance is a state that even destiny doesn't maintain. The scene is different at every waking moment. Each one may seem like the first. Some are distorted. Some seem to repeat. Constrained. Like the illusory diorama inside my skull. My mental self-portrait loitering.

---

A tongue strikes the screen, this tongue is genderless,
crude, dirty, hideous: wash me, the rainbows you place
over my jaw as your bat-winged heroine runs over the
floor my tiara spinning above her, pulling, while
hot flutes of tears touch my lips

fruits and old roses of bitter sorrow, elixir of
midnight's shattered eye, the sun is too bright,
we might burn. My sunlit jewel of an empress,
your lyre of a face the benighted world, of
love, of joy, I am at night in a flowerworld

arabesques and picotees, I conspire with unisex bird
and child sprites to cudgel your honey-hued lips,
with baby's breath

on the tips of my boots, hotweed, peppermints of
afghani, we need not talk

when we are green, in a forest made brown against my
cool, delusory torment, all mine is a hollow until the
shell, wheezing, falls dead from my green throat,
this is a forest fire.

Soft lilies cold water flowering flesh, bitter arabica,
hairy bellflower fruiting genitals

in a paroxysm of acidity to bloom the tetrameter
of my uneasiness, blancmange of opposites

and where were you then

a quadratic equation of beauty in the polytope of
the flux

vacuole and tooth of the fleecer

loose the wayward one word braid of bile

this is cool and playful, camped upon the corpse of
your nation, dark sweet roots of palm growing beneath
your feet, I reveal that limescent obituary for your
language

an unfurling twilight in the place of meaning

polyhedra stripped to nacre, within me and you,
real between my great green tickled ears, what is
"you" but some part of me that I am not

petals in my mouth, bay and dick and dirk me with
your aspidistra daggers, vilification, heel along
the lapis empandies azure of our way for her

yellow brick, brachii gratissimum, hinge metallically

softwood as gay as the arctic night, she begins to cry,
threshing me in silver waves, remnant, mass-orphaned
all

of passion, an ellipsis of incest, our dance of breath
and fizz the ballets of celluloid, masked doves and the
flat-foot serenade of milk geese

finger of wicker burnished impenetrable wall of faun
and summer, your eyes naked, heaving, heaving...

In the blue woods, well upon the hilly side is the
salting to hear your beautiful moan I'll make that
trumpet blast, your mouth of pink melon, the portal to
my image's part of the star-cuttings that frame it

basked in the whimsy of autumnbuds broken on the
inside, of a sacrilege unfurled, out of the tube,
in a nightfall, dejected from the tunnel, on an orb of
drifting cartouches

I lisp and gurgle and hiccup with the prune-streaked
rest of my ethereal climax; I am back among the people,
I am a part of the people

I am too young to understand that I am in the desert
of possibilities with no choice but to submerge

or float, depending on my position, and this is where
I have entered the wormhole of Now

forgotten a previous density, embraced another, lost
myself. I am the whole given undifferentiated mass.

When I awoke the first morning after I lived that
hellish alchemy with the force of the sun, a bullhorn
crooning, "The present is the sum of all memories."

Journey the tide of pages to acclimate our assuagement?
Bend? Dance to the tickling of lianas twining us to the
waltz of the moon?  I need to be incited by you, as if
pulling the sky into me. Am I being foolish? So be it.

For revolution is the bare root of death, the whole
for the form is change, slowly will I learn to love
the whole, this too is a pilgrimage, but not without
torture.

Thus, I'll have no country, no land, no weapon, and
this will be the most terrifying revolution of them
all, the revolution of love.

The light in the classroom is low, the windows are fleecy grey and outside it's snowing. I am thirteen and sitting in History class and notice that I brought the wrong textbook but it's too late and the bell rings and the students are seated and the teacher enters the room. In front of me is a math book and not long after the teacher begins her lecture she is looking bored and is speaking over our heads and I'm thinking about why I am here and why the teacher is so bored and I'm looking through the book of math equations and diagrams and I want to stand up and raise my hand to speak, to ask a question but I don't because they'll probably laugh at the question and I'm in this classroom and I am getting an erection but nobody notices except for this one boy sitting behind me who smiles. The teacher stands and starts talking about something else and I'm thinking about my erection but the textbooks and the lessons won't make it go away and I'm afraid I'm going to cry. And inside, I do.

The teacher calls the name of the boy who's sitting behind me and the teacher's suddenly paying attention to him and I wonder if he knows what's happening to me and it doesn't matter because I know this isn't real but it does matter and the math book slips from my hands and I'm afraid the teacher will notice I brought the wrong book. She is lecturing about war and my erection is growing larger. I wish the boy behind me would speak up but he's so scared I think he might cry and everyone else is staring. The teacher makes a joke about the boy behind me maybe being a fan of the Broncos and I have to look at him to see the smile he's wearing. I think of the word "fan" and I want to say it out loud but I don't because he's going to get in trouble for talking and I don't want to get him in trouble. I can't say "I'm a fan of you." to him. Everyone says the boy behind me looks just like me but I know that he is different or challenged or lonely or that he hates his parents and I think he's embarrassed and I'm embarrassed that people say we look alike and I wonder why the boy behind me doesn't speak up. I can't tell if it's accidental or not, but his knees keep bumping against my buttcheeks through the square hole in the back of the chair and it's just making things worse.

Opposite the windows and perpendicular to the chalkboard that the teacher sits in front of there is an old plaster wall illuminated by the granular play of snowfall and winter light. On the wall the teacher has a large framed portrait of Adolf Hitler. On the wall behind me are posters of gladiators in the Roman Colosseum and Renaissance paintings and the American Revolutionary War and ancient pyramids and a man on the moon. There are quotes from Martin Luther King, John Lennon, Anne Frank, Gandhi and the Dalai Lama. I want to leave but I don't want to be the one that gets noticed. And so, I sit there, my pants now wet with my own precum. I think of the boy behind me and I wonder if he knows that we're doing the same thing and I wonder if he likes it. I don't want to let him know that I know. I'd rather him think I'm a fan of him and not of Hitler. I don't want to be a fan of either. I wish I was brave enough to tell him how I feel, to leave me alone and I wish I wasn't so scared.

I focus on the poster of gladiators on the wall. They are contorting their faces into strange shapes and trying to convince members of the audience to enter the arena to fight. The words "I'd fight for you" appear in bold, white letters. A spear with blood drizzling from its tip flashes in and out of view. I want to feel the blood falling on me. The blood of the gladiators. I wish I could see the posters on the walls better. I think the boy behind me must be a gladiator. He's fighting to stay alive. Fighting for what? What I don't know. I only know what I would do if I was brave enough. What would I do if I was brave enough? If I had the courage? Would I be willing to sacrifice myself for his fame? I wouldn't. No. I wouldn't. I wouldn't be a hero. I would just die. It would be easier. I think about the boy behind me and how he might fight for me. If he were brave enough to fight. I think about turning around and whispering *CALIGULA* in his direction. And seeing myself in his features, I would die in his place. The quotes conjure in me a different reality altogether. The quotes conjure in me images of martyred saints and genteel angels like I'd seen in church. The quotes conjure in me the questions I think but never say. The boy behind me continues to move his knees against my behind.

The teacher is still talking and I watch her lips. Her lips form the words: "The Horseman rides". I can't tell if she's alluding to the boy behind me being a fan of the Denver Broncos football team or to the end of the world. I look to my left and hear the papery sound of two girls whispering to each other and I make out the words: "Purity/Cult", "Ethnocentric", "Nationalism", "Virtue". I think the girls are talking about Hitler but they could be talking about an organized religion. I want to jump up from my seat and run away but I can't because I'm afraid I might not be able to get out of my desk. It is a vintage American-made golden oak school desk and I am slightly overweight and the erection is starting to hurt. The classroom smells like chalk dust, old wood and disinfectant. I want the teacher to stop talking and I'm afraid to ask the boy behind me to stop because it might create a conflict or worse, someone might ask me why I'm so attracted by Hitler and I'll have to explain that my erection is not about the end of the world or Martin Luther King or pyramids or the Nazis or the boy's knees.

The teacher is still speaking and I see her say the word "separation". I wonder if she's talking about separating the boys in the classroom from the girls or maybe she's talking about Jewish people or Gay people or the African slave trade or the Native Americans or any kind of people that are different from her or from the Nazis. I wonder why the teacher doesn't have pictures of cowboys in the room. I decide to put my math book back in my backpack and notice graffiti on my desk that reads "AIDS SUCKS" and beneath that: "FAG". My eyes roll back into my head. I throw the book on the floor and sit up in my chair, adjusting my penis to a more comfortable angle.

The classroom door opens and the school nurse and a janitor enter the room. The janitor turns the lights off completely. I look down at my desk and as my eyes adjust I see graffitis of cartoonish penises drawn in ink. I want to take a pen and draw circles on the foreheads of everyone in the room. In the dark, past the shadows of the sitting students the nurse calls my name. I know it's time, I know I must go. I turn my body slowly to get up. I put my hands up on the top of my desk. I know that if I don't go with her I will probably be written up for acting out. I would like to hide the erection but don't want to reach in my pants. I am not ashamed of my erection because it is a secret like my virginity and the boy kneeing my butt. I get up, grab my backpack and the math book and approach the nurse. I can barely make out the features of her face, silhouetted as she is by the doorframe opening onto the brightly lit hallway. She slowly holds out her hand and in it appears a permanent black marker.

As I take the marker the nurse leans towards me and whispers in my ear: "The medical name for the problem you are having is *priapism*." Her breath smells like peppermint. In front of the teacher, the boy, the whispering girls, the janitor, the nurse and the other students I hold the marker and walk towards the large picture of Hitler. I look at his face. I can see my reflection in the glass of the frame, the grey light on my hair and my skin, and I look younger than thirteen. When I get to the portrait, I carefully hold the marker between my teeth and I press it against his eyes. The marker feels hot in my mouth, like a torch. I watch his black pupils dilate, his irises pucker and contract. In the faint grey light I continue to slowly and tranquilly drag the marker outward from the eyes in a curve becoming gradually further from the center until the hypnotic trajectory of the black line collides with the edge of the wooden frame and with a loud click I lose hold of the marker between my teeth and it falls to the ground. I bend over and pick it up, wiping the spit off my chin and I hold the marker outward from my body toward the class as if it is something sacred and say quietly: "The Horseman rides."

After I'm done I show the nurse. She stares at the picture for a while, and then she smiles at me. I smile back. She takes my hand and leads me toward the door as the janitor turns the lights back on. "It was easy" I say. "I just saw the horse in the room and it made me think of riding."

Watching us leave, the teacher's face tells me that it is not easy for her to laugh.

In the hallway, the nurse lets go of my hand and says delicately, "Go home...". I walk to my locker. My erection has now subsided and my mind is calm and lucent. The heavy bell rings and the hallway fills with the bodies and voices of students and I notice that the snow outside the open windows has begun to melt and the sky is a deep indigo and the birds in the naked branches of the trees are beginning to sing.

"Salivation On All Meanings, For All Occasions":

De Propaganda Fide Nobi Spiritus Sancti I.

We walk the Earth in this ancient procession, we are the smell of it, the touch of it, the taste of it. Spring gives us the incense of it, its washes, and the pain and joy of it, its small seed, born naked in the shadow of winter, shows us that it is the truth of all the seasons.

Are we crazy, I wonder, the colors so intense, the meadows, the light so naked. No. We are crazy in the best way, the way of the wild heart, the way of poets, of alchemists, of anyone who can look at the wild and know in their heart what it means. There are no other feelings in the universe. You know what it is, the secret of life, and we are the shepherds with our tears glazing our cheeks. We weep in the spring because we are chosen, because we are worth the pain, because we have been given everything, because spring is everything, because wildness is the meaning of life.

We melted in the soft lawn, made love in a bed of dandelions, had eaten the white and yellow balls with the seeds, crunched up to make milk, loved the bloom, sucked down the stem and spit it out into the road, laughing. I dropped a couple on the wall, let them dry, returned to them on the pillow where they had fallen, I looked onto other trembling green and gold heads, I found their future, and I felt it, their texture, smelled their past, the haunting of their presence. The heads of the dandelions reminded me of how things can be lost, and how a dream can come from something small. It was all ours, what we found.

They called me the World, said I was everything, even the sea, the stars... the countryside on fire. To the spring, to the summer, to the winter and fall, and to the fire, I will spit to you, I spit to you. I spit on me. When you are finished with me, or with your country, or with mine, or with yourself, I spit.

I spit love into the eye of history.

I am too old to swallow science, too old to choke on compassion.

Someone invented a new god to account for everything, for all the numbers that never add up.

I spit my death.

I spit my parents, I spit my friends, I spit in humanity's eye, where the sun blinks toward the death of a god.

I spit the ghost of the law, the reason for the end.

I spit in history's mouth, can't spit in the mouth of death, death spit out the jizz which gave it birth, death spit out the jizz of democracy.

There is no longer a western empire but I spit anyway, the empire's spit is all gone.

Three birds rise from the boughs of a walnut tree, two blue, one green. I lift one by the neck, carry a blue one in my hand, the green one I set on the ground.

The blue bird bites me as I hold it.

Death is the law of revolution. So spit, my friends. I cannot give you the answer.

Spit in the bath with the gauze like the bread of St. Paul, teeth and phlegm are spit out, left behind, spit in your cup, I'm drooling red tears, into the bowl of my nation's heart. My love runs towards you. Where do you want to go my love?

It's time to dance, in the water, to spit on the aspergillum. When I'm asked by someone, what is my motto? I spit in their face.

Spring blew a cloud of pink wild blossoms from the trees, blanketed the ground with the meadow plants gone to seed, dead stems in the dark shadow of the fallen leaves, brought a bushy limb of goldenrod. I rubbed my skin with the sharp green heads and the sticky gold of the petals, looked up into the rose-bud collar, watched the petals fall like candy onto the lawn, picked one to put in my mouth, which did not taste of flowers, in fact it tasted of dirt and rusted wire; but a crown of blossoms is not a crown, in fact, it's a halo.

Everything has flowered, is alive, blossoming, filthy, writhing and part of me, strange roses. Strange petals bursting.

Other flowers, magnolias, larger, heavy with voluptuous soft petals, too full to contain themselves, but a tide of leaves, like waves rolling in, cresting, a group of loblolly pines, ugly in their strangeness, a macabre mob. A hum of insects, buzz and buzz, like a wind machine, endless sounds. A swarm of blackbirds riding out a windstorm on haggard wings, each with its own buzzing call, a wind moving the bees into darkness, leaves, twigs, into the tree branches, a jumble of green as though a layer of leaves was lifted up by the fingers of God.

I felt the rose thorns digging into my scalp, saw the blood on my hands, the
tooth of a thorn ripped a piece of my hair away.

I pull back and shut my eyes, open my mouth, breathe in deeply.
And spit. Like the night, like birth.

The summer fireflies light the way for me, I can reach out and feel them
touch my fingers, squeeze them, caress them. Sun breaks down the color of
all things, moonlight shows through the blood, stills the storm, in the middle
of it, summer solstice, I'd trade all the summer's pleasures for a glimpse of
such truth. I'd seen the spirit of the solstice land on the windowsill, now
I just needed to believe.

I was sore, wept in the grass, spit ran the length of my chin, I held up
the blossom as one would a feather, and I bit into it, sucked the calyx,
the stem, said the flower was as real as it felt, put my forehead to the
remains and closed my eyes, and the rasping smell of death and flowers
washed over me as I grated the thorns, and I was spent, so tired I cried.

No more will come out. Tears on my cheeks, I collapse against them,
go to sleep, fall into dreams and fold into myself, like a flower.

In the morning the redbud spilled pink, like a queen, pure, round, lit from within, and I have been seeing red. Its fruit is equally as beautiful, with a wide-toothed green pouty mouth on its apex. A queen, perhaps? What kind of foolish thing am I thinking? A queen from whose tiara you could lose an eye? Do not forget, the redbud is only blossoming right now, it does not yet know the dangerous path of its life, the part of its bloom that will soon be gone and only then will it, at the very top of the branches, begin to part and take on the shade of tears. No no, not yet, not yet.

There is a smell that comes off the earth after a rain, something sweet and far away, something impossible to describe but I know it when I smell it. To the Gods of Boredom, take a leaf from my dirty hand. I do not believe in flowers but I do believe in girls with flowers in their hair. I've never had any room to be sentimental with love, but the joy in my heart is earnest, and I cannot be sad or lonely when I am sitting with love. The sacred nature of love made all of these wet, slimy little miracles of flowers, their bright and slimy sweetness down inside of me as well, and I breathe it into the rest of my body, like a sigh.

We fell into a patch of foxglove, our buttocks stained with an oil of goldenrod. We fell, sucked the spores of penicillium into us, sweat rolled into our buttocks, we copulated in the dirt, grass clippings, perfume, mushrooms, muddy milk. We made ourselves daisy crowns, the tiniest chains dripping at the throat of a dead sky. I will tie my hands to the tree to prove I have not lied. Against the tree, you will flagellate me with all of the hatreds you have for the perjurers of a fallen world.

Love lies like a whisper down the hill, off to the left of the road, leaves me with the ivy halo in my hand. Like the child in the painting. It glides past like a breeze. It's gone, but I know it's out there, still it will whisper to me, it whispered in the night when I was my best. I am still, I must say. The longer I wait, the harder it will be when I get it back. My love lies like a whispered feather. It tucks me in, wings me and sings to me until the night comes and the moon takes over, takes the shapes of the landscape away, erases the contrasts until all is the color of bone.

Black shorn grass we turned into teeth and tongues, leering eyes and huge yellow and orange mouths that held our seed. Blue wild grass into mandibles, tusks, tentacles. We found our truth, and were united, rutting madly in wildflower meadows, rubbing and releasing, dust and seeds flying.

We danced the tiny and large, the wild and everything in between, kissed, purred, murmured and found a tombstone shaped like a heart, we fucked on fresh graves in that tenebrous space, for all who had died there. We heard sounds, the stillness of the water and the wind and the owls, we all jumped and we fell, we drank our death and we floated back to life, to shore, on the way up to the canopy of the trees where I woke up, cold in the coppices of hazel, field maple, sweet chestnut and lime, but with a smile, drenched, becoming spring itself.

In a midnight birch, I reach for the branch, snatching a flower, closing my eyes as I bury the kiss, taste the bloom with my eyes shut, the flower is raven silk and the flower smells like sex and death and I inhale the perfume of the flower and the seed and hold the stem with a gentle hand. I spilled into a flower, cleaned up after. This is what joy is, isn't it? I said to it. More. Faster. The bell and the zinnia and the iris and the glint of the forest, my fingerprints and moony blood and seed on the petals.

It's lightening now, outside of all the places I've been, dreams, prayers, this hour. What was it about the Earth? How different it is at night. I couldn't shake the chill from my belly as I stood naked in the hot sun as night turned to day. I felt as if I had been splitting myself into sun and moon, and the Earth was the dreamworld I inhabited, a series of rooms, passages. I was the wild, the Earth was the wild.

I let the Earth push against me, knees bending to the horizon. I felt the Earth's despair, loss and pride and exhaustion and glory. I imagined being an Earth, being at the mercy of the sky, of the rain, of my own anatomy. I was the stone feeling love, no matter how much I hurt myself, no matter how cold my longing. We were warm in the loss of ourselves and the wonder of becoming. The rocks digging into our ribs.

I had watched the sun rise over the glens, the woods, the clouds going from a dark blue to a bright orange, clouds mimicking the orchids I pulled, breathed and smelled, and the orchids reminded me of my childhood, I could sit for days at a time listening to the geese settle down, I'll draw them, like a child, make them more real, I'll write scribbled sentences to hold the shape of them. Find oolong seed pods and twist them, add all of them to a jar with rosemary, holly leaves, and vinegar. Capture the essence of anything you can think of, and I'll write them down in a thick ledger of words with indexes at the back. Feverish yet indeterminate, the dollop of aniseed in one's eye.

I stroke the symmetry of a flower with my tongue, the tongue of my flower with my lips. I am not a person of great emotion, I barely feel these things. I feel the weight of my perfume, the gentleness of my slender fingers against the stem. I lay the opening of the petals between my teeth, let their sweet pollens pool with my spit, let the spherules fall out of my mouth into a little river — a milk river, a honey river.

I feel the gale force of the wind, and the sky surrounding us, the sky and the trees, and the sun, wandering down to the ocean collecting starfish in the tide pools. Their pink matted bodies bruised my fingers, the urchins pricked me and I cried, unapologetic tears. I made every moment count, each insect, each bird, each fish, each creature, each wave.

The world is saturated with metaphors and similes, nature is frantic with them, they dance through me like a wind, in and out of the air, pushing up my hair and my body back to the fields, we got on with it, the sex dewiness of it, the desire, the violence of it, the hirsuteness. I lick the sweet head of a daisy, my tongue raw, smelling of dung I laughed at myself, climbed back out into the world wet with soil and spit and manure caking my hands, inhale the delicate souls of the roses, let them slip through my fingers, let them fill my lungs until the sacs sting and I can almost taste their smell, so close it's almost bitter, so close it's almost sweet, so I never forget. Inhale the joy of grass. Deep and long. Inhale the nectar of lilies, delicate and sharp. Let them swallow me up, I know them, this temperature, too well.

Crisp grey days and patches of pure white clouds are the cutest things I have ever seen, especially when contrasted by the sun, this slow march of the jessamine knicking at the haze. I breathe in this sweet citrine rain, the smell of eucalyptus, the smell of a real spring rain. I have been waiting for a real spring rain all my life.

Some things don't change, or we never changed, could never change, the ways my mind runs, the things that put it together, the things that tear it apart.

I am not going anywhere. I am sitting in the grass, I am watching the petals of a verbena curl and grow. My chest heaves from a little laugh. I plant calendula in damp ground, dusting and scrubbing the flowers in clove tea, fingers smeared with dirt and feces, hit onto their waxy surfaces, I fed them barley, stroked the crowns, turned the flowers once in the dappled sun, then twice in the darkening shadows. Begged the weeds, from the field, which felt like loving my mother, from where I held my face up to the wind, until the stubs of green with bloomers were plucked and I can hear it in my mind, hear it in the night, a yell of laughter, an exclamation: *I love you.*

Spring came to give us everything, in the great satisfaction of this slow ecstasy, this invisible ecstasy in wildflowers, and where there are flowers there is us, there is a breeze, there is a rising and falling of petals and insects, people and animals, hovering dreams come true, the cats sleep and the dogs run and the rain falls down from the clouds. Where there are flowers there is spit.

I reach out my arms, feel the soil, the steaming midden, gather handfuls, mix them in my mouth to bloom, then cake my breast, my thighs, down to the feet and I taste the compost, sweet and dying, I taste the nectar, fleshy red and fresh, clean and utterly delicious. It's only from the night, last night. From yesterday, we smelled like a cattle corral, a putrid hog pen, a zoo… the smell of life, when I didn't want to go back inside, I scooped the dirt with my thumb and put it in my mouth, tasted it on my tongue.

Through nothing but grace, Spring at its most lovely, fat bell flowers veined with purple and freckled with silver, a cascade of a hundred bees crowding in a single teardrop of black trumpet shaped salpiglossis, a lunar bouquet of the columbine. My little dove, they will steel your name, but you will always be you. I can barely breathe. The moon rose the same color as a stained glass window and the trees lining the hillside, stark in their ochre fullness, crossed over the pavement in a dark arch, they carry the seeds of my imagination, these islands of my imagination looking out onto great vacuous expanses.

My heart was beside itself, my night was burning with flowers. I was walking in the fields, I was dancing in fields, not knowing the time of day, I was a lunatic under my queen, dripping bloody spit, dreams of lilacs enfolding me in a geometry of purple smoke.

I walked through fields of daffodils, sharpest spring light blowing red petals like icing off black cake. I touched the stub of wood left from a bird feeder, said thank you to the tufts of moss, dipped my fingers into the sleeping Earth. Rubbed the Earth, fed the Earth.

I took the cicadas out of the ground and put them in my mouth, one at a time, wet their tiny hibernating bodies between my lips and roof of my mouth, smiling into them, the hills turned charcoal green, struggling to tell day from night, the air was brown with dye. I drank the crushed bodies, sucked out the juices and the minerals, kissed my fingers and rubbed their winged husks on my body, scrubbed myself with meadowsweet.

I wore the leaves of skunk cabbage, wore the fetor into a field of yellow. I sifted through the heavy ovules of a giant hydrangea, licked out the nectar. I walked through the silence of the night. They are afraid of us, these animals, they know the danger we are to them, the danger they are to us. They sense it, they know that I know it too, so many of us, such is the texture of lives, delicate and fierce, deadly but so precious, offering ourselves up to the vigor and rot of the world.

Our mouths full of yarrow, sucking the spines of brackenweed, a dragonfly's eggs dripping onto our teeth. The forgotten amanita, the wild garlic, the green millet, the hare's wiry whiskers. Eyes parted, our swollen lips compressing, planting ourselves in a hollow, sowing the seeds of these flowers into our flesh, absorbing them as life, bringing them into every corner of us so we will never wither.

I'll wear their colors, their textures, their smooth cellulose masques. I'll fall asleep against a lily's curled throat, I'll lay my head against the crook of an elm, hear the milling of the wind in the tall grass. I opened my mouth, like a flower in the sun, I kissed the rosebuds, their color more luminous than the pink sugar on my lips, their breath of taste stronger than the blood of my sex. I saw the color of the sun in its open petals, and then when it came out through my lips, as fast as my tongue raked the cupid's bow of my pixie-strawberry iced lips at a half-loud giggle every way and I tasted a single speck of strawberry syrup.

Poplars painted in deep purple, crisscrossed with honeysuckle, I walked barefoot, my footprints hidden in the dirt and umber. The crows gathered above the stalks, watched me climb, picking and twirling into grass, I love the taste of grass, of Spring, I love everything I am made of. I brought these flowers inside and I ate them, I ate them all, I spread the grains of the stamens, I ate the bulbs, they smell like snow, there is a taste like tasteless fabric, and a dry piece of bloodless meat, like iron filings melting into water.

Tiny white irises, drifts of lilac, cotton candy pink-and-blue roses, leathery flowering clematis, I crouch, exhausted, under the branches of a white oak and watch a hawk in the sky. She cannot see me. Her wing feathers are so glossy that they look as though they have been bronzed, my knees against the bark. I don't want to call her, don't want to scare her, positioning my toes between the thick vascular roots. The way she's soaring on the winds is less the way any hawk has flown before, she's just that free, my kneecaps pressing hard into the jagged stones. She sips the waters of a stream in the woods, she drinks the cool silver of the water, my shoulder blades wrenching, sore.

I found it hard to believe that the stately old elms and weeping willows I knew only by their sound were still standing. It was obvious, some blooms had seemed out of place, but the flowers were all equal to me. And then it was morning, once again, and the air was clean, and my hair and body were heavy with the scent of flowers.

Indeed on this new morning, the tulips had much to be riled up about. Now upon return, each and every plant, shrub, or tree continued its blossom, the violets and the foxgloves and the vetchlings that dotted the sides of the road into the city. Soft cornflower petals glowed through an even blue haze, I stopped at one tree whose branches hung close to the road and caught the Spring's bright petals in a graceful blast of confetti.

In pink lipstick, I flushed the corners of my mouth, I bled each trace of syrup through the petals, in the sugar of pale sunlight, I kissed these flowers on the lips, told them they were the most beautiful, the sweetest things I'd ever seen.

The air, thick with pollen, is golden, the sun is white and hot. We had nothing but the flowers, they had little power, but they gave it to us anyway. We threw their tears in phials, felt their madness in our blush and in our bellies, we heard their songs. We did everything we could to coax them back into bloom, to bring back the glory of their past, their future, no difference.

The pollen is thick in the air, pink, yellow, orange, red. My eyes burn. I found you in the Spring, found you and nursed you with all the things the ground gave me: sap, honey, mud. They stroked me tenderly, the blades beneath my feet. I slept with you in the cocoon of my mouth, my breath one of your blue windows, my lips against you dripping pearl spit, your soft gauzy body cool in the hollow of my throat, your velvety mouth kissed me.

We took our rest and watched the dawn, the violet sun turns the tulip into a cathedral of vanity, white flowers hung with raffia red, under my breast the yellow daisy cuts into my lip. I drip a few white petals, taste their floral lisp, taste the oil of my tears. I kiss the daisy on the lips, lap my tongue over the trillium's throat, taste its flower tongue. I crush the trillium's ear into my lips and imagine the way it rings. I swallow it whole, leaflets rimming the burned out blossom of my mouth.

All we had to be was the wind and the Spring and the heart and the Earth. We made love in its name, through its form, into its bones. I reach out into the darkness and feel the trees trembling in it. All this for me, all this for us.

I buried this one. The song I made for it began to drown. I gaze at it, a field of blue with lights to let in the sunset, a circle of orange, a symmetrical halo around my head. The tulip breathes. I close my mouth to catch its brilliant petals. I touch my eyelids, I keep them closed, I am holding the tulip in my throat and gently, gently I force it down. I don't want to swallow, I want to hold it, I want to hold the blossoms in my body, I want to resurrect them, to be resurrected, forever. I gag and think of keeping it, keep it in my mouth as a bright replica, keep the pollen that flickers like fire in the air like rain forever burning in my lungs.

My legs spread, tied to a sickly linden, bits of petal on the bruised upper buttocks, petals smeared down my thighs, the blossoms on my lips, sweet honey like velvet on my tongue, dew on my pelvis, holding my pelvis and soiling it, the sun melting my weight into the opening ground.

I flexed in the restraints, up from the roots of the tree, I opened my ass, and I opened my eyes, I looked at the sun, and I looked at myself in the green grass, and I knew: I am as far from the brittle breastbone of winter as can be, growing new life without ever being unfurled by its pistons. I am the only one, I am the rose covered in a sweat like down, the spit rose, the bloom blanched in my snowy mouth, the tiny flakes floating like diamonds on the immaculacy of a night breeze.

I dig a hole, I pour dirt over, down into it, a circular scoop, and bury myself, bury myself deep in the soil, bury myself forever.

I drowned the tulip's memory in the dirt, inside with my face, my hair, my hands. Tiny army ants nesting in my cavities, where I begged to be alone. Tucked up in myself, found nothing much to do, just breathing, retracting inward, I pet the heads of snails, I rub dirt in my mouth, dirt in my eyes, insect larvae, dark-winged fungus gnats. I wrap you in my mouth and bury you in the dirt, gently now, for a moment or two, for my flower, for us both.

Every blade, every stem, every petal, every seed, and my body, all mingled up into the mud of one color, the one order of this superseason, this emotion, this bright horizon of felicity.

Under the trees the rocks were limestone, soapstone or basalt, the moss new and shiny, the lichen singed white. When we felt we had grown too lethargic, so many blossoms, I drenched my naked body in water, worked myself back into it. I smelled a blooming organ, I crawled back to the cleft in the rotted log where I had first tasted it, I smell the hot weeping of the bud as it emerges, clear, I squeeze my nipples like miniature flowers, I stand under the water; I feel a viscous, ethereal flow.

Look at the tree, the bird, the river, their songs come roaring out of me, I hold them all, the stream so close. I see it again, the azalea, the snapdragon, the iris, the lamb's ear. As if each windblown bough is searching, it knows something you cannot, it knows something new, I know it.

I pull the hard skin off a bunch of rhubarb and eat it until I am shaking, vomit on my own hands and knees, vomit on the brush, even the trail, everything is dry and bristles, and there was a scent of warm stones and it has been that way ever since. I make myself a mistress of the small acorn, one that refuses to become a World Tree unless the attention of humanity is upon it. My shell is fragile and I hope the inner brilliance will be up to the challenge.

Sabotage committed, I would serve it with gout in the bitter vomitus not without a nobler circumstance. I was never the same after that, and that night the light was silver-white and you were there. Wiping my mouth with your tongue, as we bled the aniseed, anise is my semen, which is semen only insofar as it is the history of our love. I saw my own face in the flesh of a delphinium, I caressed the delphinium's arms, kneeling before it.

Shades of pink were rising to meet me. Without my knowing, without my thinking, without any will of my own I ripped the flower from its roots, pulled myself off the flower's stem, the dust carried down my arm, from my elbows, and my legs and I wept as the sun weeps through me, through the liquid of my body, and the sun is death and the dead are my sweaty lovers, and there is still plenty of time to love and this is not loving it is making love, I squeeze the first petals of Spring between rubbled surfaces, my lips closing on a white bell's phallus and it's shooting me wide open.

Then I lick a couple of my fingers, I push the tips of my fingers into the soil, taste earthworm, keep it moistened with the others, slipped my teeth over the dripping bells, pulled them in, suckled, licked up the warm come. My lips slathered wet between the shafts, my hands dragged the delicate flesh around, over my breast and down my flat belly. I licked my fingers, pulled each one apart, licked the webbings clean of spit and come and the dirt and sucked them clean.

I promise you, the evening is never just a grey leafless frame when you are alone, and I would give you kisses in Spring's dismal shadow. The penumbra's static in your ears, this hellebore half-dead in the sun. Your dead tears turn to leaves, of frail gold leaf, snow covered fields become a drumhead of flaming pastels. Spring is a canoeing song whose echoes form shapes I do not understand, a drift of cabbage bladders over soft fields.

In a barrow I bury a bee, a bee whose death has been known by many, who would say I am every drop of rain that falls, every leaf, every sparrow, the brook and the sea. The other bees are quiet because my body is dyed with the funeral colors of an arctic tundra, the colors of starry gas, and the barrow is still.

I was full and the tulips were also full, and we were naked, their mouths open, their tongues flat, the smell of them resinous. Their perfume is suffocating, intense, but I want it to never stop, and I cannot stop.

I was naked, sated, I kissed the fans of arnica, I kissed the tissues of the salvia, the blossom of the shoot, I kissed the meadowfoam leaves, I love the Earth, I love us, the Earth loves us, the Earth did not want to move, not as we kissed it into the night, into the one thing, the meadow, the tree, the river, the sea, the road, the hill, the field, the garden, everything.

I clamped my nose to a nosegay of ground ivy, nuzzled it, held it against my skin, clenched my heart to its sharp leaves. I hummed the song of the heliotrope. I dug in the dirt, mired myself to my knees, painted pink by roses, bordered the irises and lilies with sticky spells, I planted the yellow pansies with their starbursts in the hollows of my belly. I crept up on a little daffodil that looked like a confection of silver, opened my mouth as if I could drink its unappetizing light, a conflagration of blooms in the ferns, I walked through the grass, along a gray lake, bringing myself back to myself. I forgot the hills, forgot the wind, forgot the trees, forgot everything. I forgot the phloxes and the crocuses and the dianthuses, scraped through a tangle of defiled laurels.

But I remembered the Spring. I remembered the world, I remembered mostly that I was alive. Mud and grass in the recesses of my flesh, a fall of slippers lace around my scabbed ankles. There is a stream behind me, there is the green of a young forest, like a winter's bruise, only a perfect meadow, paths and dead leaves and light, a dreamlike tone to all of this. I spread my wings and soar up and over the headland, take off in a rush of dry leaves, I slide down, sit back against the moss, the stone, my own private tree. I push my feet against the rock and lay back, and my head falls against the smooth bark, I push the rock, force it up, over and over, and then I sit on its lower curve, and curl into a ball.

Spring is the roaring, the surging, the crackling of the wet Earth, the flaming dawn, the sweat of it, the fierce oneness of it all. The maples drink in the light, fill their leaves with the new sun, the old drops go up, gold drops, red drops, moon drops, snowdrops, the fading color of fire, up.

We are the two that are one, we are the holy and the unholy, we are the pain of it, the happiness of it, we are Spring in the ancient myths, we are the wilderness. The wild aureole of the bright primrose and its sensuous scent; the fire as the dark ore of our malice; and in these wretchedly lorn flowers there is me, hiding my time of death from the tempest that shall wake me, my voice stripped, all brio reduced to a vow I'll make in the night, like the tendril of a dream. Perhaps as a climax.

*Alleluia*

We are these things, I see the word 'alive' everywhere, it's the root of everything, we say thank you to the wild, see what we can become, we say thank to the star, for the naked joy of death, we are one, this moment, as it passes and slips away—we say thank you, we are not two, we are one.

# Abscissa of Thistles

It is of these incites that I would be entirely
satisfied

the modern pretenders are so desperate to be loved —
*Abscissa*, be thy barometer, if you can —

Orchidea, flushed and vomitous, deliver you into this
wildbound legion of

throat-slashed saints

in the realm of faery the hidden stars that blazed
in the horror of the eye of Eve's black milk

Ossifragum, the hag's napkin

moulded from the overtures on which be cast my first
blushing bloom.

The kingdom of youth is shaped like a cloud

and our forlorn hearts are broken, by this neon-pale
elixir

though it's they who've trodden it in blood, a
thousand-colored feathered chains hang from the
tenacious thorns

that lace with the filament-pale lamb's hair, with the
smoke

of your tepid cum where the flock is whipped and
thrashed by lash and tip,

I'm the dancer's wail, the courtly freak.

To begin again, a love makes eyes like these

daughters of Isis, know the ways of plague, or no
medicine of the written word

I could not be the pioneer without you, I did not know
what I wanted, who I was

only beyond the self who is there

I felt the fever of love before I had a language for
it, before the insect kingdom, before this
Republic

but now language hath profited thee

I feel we deserve at least an equal conversation

a parallax love how the story is repeated the way
history repeats itself

a twisted thread

fragile and deathless, near the chlorophyll blackness
of our threshing —

daughters, the plague is our führer.

Militant dragonsome primus I'm engaged

to droll Englishness or so the singers say

far eclipsed this chromate ovale to renounce the
goldsmith's perineum, to rinse

the rabbit's ass I swim

the gentility of muck by bunkard hedge and shattered
dune

of this knight's ghost, he's everburning, he is
anerotically thine.

But I do have my own code, and I am named
the Angel of the Snowy Abundance

the knight's brawn scar I swim, the white apehoods of
the timescale I permeate I contaminate I transfuse
the flamberge

of their swash, the wail of fallen fiefs and

the acrostics of their crack, the restlessness of the
rank.

Foul in it, I am. Curse me not, gentle reader,

or else cast me upon the basest dunghill,

by a sticky sea of bruises made in the name of kings.

My twins sometimes crawl on these foul tresses of
malachite

either scrabbling in behind or emanating through the
drooping membranes

no dreary record in war the wastedness of the wheels

of salt beget violent haemorrhages the whites of my
eyes

vitiated in the solar catafalque's fuliginous
fullness —

had taken for your salt a heifer, take for your flint

a spider's bitch, this duodecima

will make mincemeat of me, too thick

in both weight and force to be crucified on wood, our
dead King of the Wreck shot out gold the concentric
solar hexagons

bud of your head cover its feathered bulk, as thought,
and done through a certain hoar-green phase

blooms pipped of earl's tears to mistletoe

take in every sound a caesura, become the law and
leave it impotent, waste on the futility of our vain
insect wars a dolorous doggerel

of vulture agonies in the purple house of sand.

Thrice glistening lines, ragged bows, sheaves

cotyledon downloft withdraw and besieged in feral
flight he eases in snow

on shafts of blade-white sunshine

prismed veils and the grey of ambrosia, in the swells
beyond thunders wherefore is this song?

*Oh, you know...*

Meet me there in the fireside hamlet

as your burning treacle then my lip of moons soothed
from your planar ochres, to lick the foretaste of your
waist, sun-shot honey, in the babble of birds before
the lines, the lines, the agonic lines

and cold you blew your breath on my curls, calling the
lambent flower, nestling to you for a golden milk

Here I shunt the nunciatures at the blooming thatch,
flutter to dusthooves, disperse their gossamer
wingdresses

I saw you there in the bread anons you sat in your
holland as cool as a cut lollipop

smiled, gasped and

wondered.

The roses are back

The mushrooms are back

The rodents are back

Oh! your bairn is backwards I knelt beneath the lilac
eve in a dream where the forest sang in the child's
lisp and then I saw the moon, above my tomb rose me
this night so far away I've fallen down the white road
and into a whirling mist in which I am winged and lost
and the night never ends

flowers on my lips but I know that they burn, I am the
night of smoke but I know that it's just an interlude

A

ghost most-not

Ayahuasca vine me

were I to sigh, Mother

heed my words, all fear, all doubt is interlude.

The moth fluttering from the switchblades of the
frost-killed flame: without their light there is no
night.

See! here's a small bit of the sun.

*Abscissa! Ascensi!* Three graces I draw down from
above — Woman my scorpion maiden that leaves nothing in
her wake, Queen of the

dirty dagger serene her dark coral still as a
grove of forest in earnest glowing — *O Abscissa*,
further, as spikenard and not the pollens of your
tactile devilflowers

And what of the garden blight, the fact that I, a
flower desiccated, a vase-to-rim with my fuzz ghost

will be at the top of the second balcony The Sun is My
Body

I am the one without a hair The Sun, I am a body of
water but I go out when needed The Sun is My Bath

Butterfly, I could be a processional softbeast were
it not for that persistent pest, the Bard, who for
long years now, tugs his three-fingered hands at
the hems of my gowns, battering them into tiffany
memories of white cotton candy highlands, dark eudora
foliage, toothed to the Arcadian iliastra

Remain I too in peace so sweet so rare so tender

new pranas mean reveling in the soft, terrible landing
of the sun's complete bodygraft, and still so in the
morning

the cauterizing heat of semen will set me at a boil
and glaze my eyes with night.

*O Abscissa*, wrap them up, in seaweed and sleep
until your nightmares come to court the god of fleas,
to dance at your gates with this bedraggled throng,
where again, at dusk, you'll stay forever, and as for
the plainsong melody, the organa, forget it not.

The wellspring, in all the violence of winter, I
awaken thy will, I smash the sun into my forehead,
into the tower of alphabets!

Desire has naught to do with love, whatever is,
indeed, the past and present, but there can be
something of it in the future

bleached on the desert floor to a tincture of
purity, the coyote-like urine has such heat to give
me the shivers as by this

deleterious day

You can't do more than escape, laving through
tainted tunnels and such gateway joys, your mucosal
aura always on fire, but for the reason all flames
are now spirals that blend into my milk-shot eyes so
deep, so emotional that new soils are born, and to
this extent

I prick you as you fasten the cocoon of a dead
cell to my antlers with clumsy hands, and
through the frame of my fenestrae, this is a
letting go... not so much an abandoning.

I no longer trust the masque of your scalene kiss
as sweet enough to crown my bonfire of messengers

in that I know the molten fever in you, it's cups
stinging veils, aching hairy chiffons flecking the
floor

is something I cannot resist, go ahead, glide past
me as I moan for another hour or enough now for a
speech of all that is left, as to my soul

a renunciation of the question

too full of life to repose, I ask myself:
*What is love?*

And was the knitted slipper tainted by us

as the pelt dries slowly on the pallium of a
lover's smile?

Perhaps I would dance the paeonia

*Moi-même, Abscissa a pataugé un jour…* meek once

through the foetal leaves of sleek psychotria,
numb and frail

in the sunniest of affairs, not for any reason of
strength, but to prove

that all is vanity, that even the most dainty
daffodils

can refuse to live.

My eyes cloud as smoky hues a square of flame where
I am, like a child I am dirty and they are picking
me up they helped me onto the horse. A baysnow,
brilliant and searing how they tortured his eyes —
The smokey light of the horizon from beyond, which
I saw but too late. The knife in the eye they shot at
me, the grey fire my smile and I'm sleepwalking amid
translucent threads of mirror in the night of crystal

I fear none here cowering the first hymn of passion
aloft the bath of the milk of night is below

plant the leopard slug in the balm for this
annealing rash of ghosts

you ask why I zen my grapes in black starlings, young
ghouls of the bloom

ask yourself again    why I seek

At my feet the sands are still white And like
Tristan's tears the tears of the gulls

will reveal your riot's toy, hurt at the crest will
flirt even you darling of my heart whom I wish I could
see every grain in capricious frozen premonition

Identity-stuck with a question the shape of an atom
ooze within the minuscule madronema blister of some
midwife, blueing on glistening alabaster ankles scabbed
with harp marks, the nearest thing to God. But on a
sabbath, I celebrate all who walk with God.

I run my black winter through the combed-back grains
of you, stringing from your blood quill with tear-dwarfed
kachinas, from head to tail, the geomatic prisma
predicating calligraphy, impasto.


Now too does my itching cocoon spread itself


and drip into the infinite steel of a venous
emmanuel


the mirror-glinting reptile of aquas


deemed by me to be the nova-eyed father-son in
these shadows of intarsia


caterpillar cheeks riven in citrus rind on
high-sparkling aureoles


I plant my silver fireworks in the wet scum on
my name when a ballerina sweats the colour of
daisy fields, elsewhere I am all that is left and
nowhere the waiting gauze mounds of dirty butcher
hands flytrap my bare void, nox the pathe
of my barren halls to caress the cardinalis.

A sense of emptiness alone compels me, un-confident

(but not without pride), lonely…


No word, again

to render the saxifrage and the blue-shirted adolescent

on her porch steps

seeing: it's hard to keep track of this state, another

lipsticked mouth. Twilight on her thorax the

yellow chevron of the sun

spinning

until:

flash flood, roar, a dragonfly ballerina

flailing

— who's this girl, in the collapsed mouth of the night,

who knows the whole poem: A boy with no words, I run

around the country from farm to forest to swamp

the families of ravens my family, the swans awake

the people awake, and waiting

for the bedsheets to lift their tears

as they flail along with the hangovers, the blind

dogs, the beggars — everyone is up and waiting for the

sheet to go up

on this Ghost : no empty spaces

no Who Am I

When I go behind the rim, of the marshes to obliterate
in one cathartic rush all of the whitehot magnesium
slugs who hunted you in the night

or the fine loose hairs by somersault, handstand of
pummeled blue cream? Snot shattered nectary of damaged
matter I exist by taste

my madrigal of punctuation is the crack in this cement
Eden

It's just a garden, but I don't know how to look at
this land, to see this landscape: where the
ceaseless fuses of the candle are stabbed and osmose,
the breccia which drips inside my head, onto
the vernixes of pukey green ferns.

No spotlight here, my littoral incantations to the
twilight, like a fingernail on black paper, such a
methodical tide of unique interlocking connotations,
where my meniscus pulses in hyacinthine treble
a conlang I conglominate my own catacomb of forces
into arachnid predynastic maxims.

I could crush you to my cellular concept of the
sun, I think: 'How could one say what is the image
of the sun in the prolepsis of spider eyes?' White
cataclysms of mortal snakes! Hah! Such childlike
naiveté and despair.

There is no doubt it was I who mounted the horse in
riding to my murder

provoking what was never sated in the parricides

an apical tiner, blyed in velvet

or maybe the prophets have left me to their whims only
by presupposition —

Our act is a play my lemon in your mouth voiding body,
elytrons cover our forms

time has crusted them with green-rotten glitter.

Come words, so and you, come from my delicate throat
the petrous pendant of a lemon torn wide-open
to reveal the putrid infusions, into the opening
swells of pink sluice calyxes to climb, you, ripe and
wet thorn her eyes to the terpene tops

where the sand be even with the bones my sister of
fern she in locusts her

dark and pert and forlornly veiled, at the end of the
deep valley

I'll wake in my castle-hell and assume corporeality,
they'll lick my leprous thighs with bat tongues

I did but thirst there in the dark the white swan is
your eyelashes spilling

like a chocolate milk of aphids

she says call her Aleph but we know how the
crocodile bites glow hot as you bathe me

you don't say *Goddess* but some faint moonlight
overbraids her

into the soft apparition of marble, not the one from
the womb of Africa

that can whisper with words a wordlessness the reason

why God was not lost in that forest of the mists on
shifting shelves

the cubit of Lilith is an anagram

Fingers pointing in my direction, I spy the foot of a
ruler

tortured into surrendering an inferior skinned moon
in its rest

And you the runt fish go screaming to escape the
meretricious hues.

Between you and me I want the cremastery of your
self-generated heat

deterged with incest the passion sliding on the
script, pushed from the green ice-slush of my
anus

out into the world, the secret Deep wants to
come out

in an incomprehensible purge. And to be silent

in that noise

is to be nowhere

destroying their presidiums, I offer my
vorpal
invocations to the non-word

Roma, Roma from there, wherever eyes grope the
vatic emblem of private ritual; akin to
inseminating a twin of the sun

the puma spits out her calves but needs
twentyseven cartloads of moss for the star's
branched throat

No dove hath ever sexed a crone so knickerless

Would you hold me then, with and without formula?

See how Abscissa opens doors

to save one from an imperious control

this is the birth, and the release

peeling back what has been lost in this scabbed
oasis of magpies

an insectigram unkindly, leeling with trust in its
dawn-eye

so much for lust's sweet whisper

broiling to lastness the burnt palate of puckered
blood-melon, or maybe a soft brush of velour and
I'll let it go

give me a muse within the geometrical fusion of
ash

let the tears of Atlantis rattle through the
scissure.

Sciences conned from separate chambers of my
brain where wisdom is not exiled, and no
frontotemporal dementia can rob me of who I am

Cloud shadows in a tumble of lace of ostrich and
advocaat satin and zebra-print pyjamas of almond
silk, valentine madness as vulval sonnetry in
verdigris

your paint will dry to blood-rust on my lionhearted
cleft deckled as a Carpathian rose face embossed
with honeybeams, while, abreast

my request for orchids that still, in hot yellow
mists yawn into the agora of smoke and stucco as
this most eccentric saint

flashing palma the pap of my scabs, asceticite

toasts to Albrecht Dürer, and leaves as a viscosity
a seed up of chocolate tears, the longman the
flag of those who straight are slaughtered and
the littlest log the guerilla coat of pine
branches

blundering through the whitehooked emerald veins
of a Midlothian sky.

Harmony, harmony, while I dream the eyes under my eyes
cannot peer

at the stars am I not a sphinx to feed you with intervals,
to play with the babbling pool of meadow patterns in the
starlight, love is everywhere if not it's wildly splotched
by death or a pale ghost

I like to unearth languid zones and scaraboid crests, my
perusal of the pulse works their universal agent on the
violet riot of sparks

I garland the palorine with torn endoscopes and I learn
myself to murmur and nuzzle at my almond vagina, as if
it were a deserted orb which does not affect you, though
your emotions are lost in these limpid golden prolifera

the cancers of prisms of sibyls of irascibilities of your
latest appurtenances, of extinguished sexual alleles—
O come like a surge of throes, within the bodies of wilted
Alhambras, illimitable, polished and tendentious, quetzal
flats they bleed from my boots in polluted beds my lover
in peace my lover in peace

She's really no different from all the rest, I know where
you're going, twinkle, twinkle, the burst of a blooming
berry glitters from her tamarisk grove, braces of blue
blooming amygdalines, her nostrils exude a fog of dead
hares in shimmering session, she is the fire of the
morning foam

*Abscissa, murmur, declare, edelweiss, magnifique.*
*Abscissa!*

It is not the masque of my name

that confronts you today

on the steps of dolmen floors for the thirteenth
night of the Lupercalia

the woodchuck bloat'd, but not on any gauge of the
apricot's welt

in earnest, for such is the habitantry of nature's
grace

blistered on ragweed and the fat acupoints of
question marks, trying to stretch a swath of
parsecs on bone brooches

To myself I say

Belong to a transgression where each fleck in the
white of your tear's skull is not the juice

that drips from the eye of a monkey god

tell your flowers to kiss my death with the blue
oil of henna, even after your flagstones bleed so
stained a ginkgo's sap

with turquoise ants of madness.

Tulips in piss stinking bedsides into the willow grove,
I meditate squatting weftwise along the brook, watching
this nymph,

turn her back on the morning of All the Light of
Christendom

*belle soleil,* then bright and clear

singing this there's love to this my astrologica, and
the arrow in the lake's skin the thrash the thrash
I saw that mountain I saw that mountain I saw that
mountain

in a splay of datura the sepals of blood will hiss and
the mangle of my blushes should blaze under the
outermost canicules

vestments a vassal has shed in front of a king
redly highlighting the dehiscent body, like a

badge should inspire scorn as empress of the forest my
eminent clowning queen

*Abscissa*

In what shape a centipede upon your blood geometry

frozen princess on its back through the night
glowing with midnight sparks

Frozen rabbit like a painting of insanity wrought
by Columbine & Freja

spilling the tvblood of eyes

through this hemlock the force is bound, something
like ascertaining

the poppies closing the scroll of time that
confides in the varietal

of thorns, of disconsolate thistles

the same text of waxing and waning reigns
sonorous, miraculously reborn into iterations
unto its end.

*Abscissa!*

# THE DUSK OF NEW VENUS

Lilith  Sugared  and  New

Honesty ——————————————————— Head

## <u>CLOSER TO THE MOUTH OF GOD</u>

Covetous  Muse

I'm          here!          I'm          there!

The Odyssey,                Mythopoeia

Autumn-White, —————————————————————

————————————————⟩ I always meet myself
coming  and  going   and  if  we
should  meet,  would  we  not  find
that  we  have  always  been  there
in  winter,  getting  high  with  the  slimy
salt  slugs  on  your ——————————————
bascinet ——————————————————————

On the road                                    out
            to the mesa, little stalks with bright
red, blue, or violet spikes in the center

Superficial  ~~Gilgamesh~~  Semilunar eyes

Because you lied to me, I fell down

Burst  into  lemon  sunshine  in  a  meadow

| I. | I will find you, barefoot in the field |
| II. | The King in Flaming June |
| III. | Phthalo-platonic/hermetic, paraclete sissy, demigod |
| IV. | your Flaming June goes on forever. |
| V. | Watch me thread its bloody skein through your fractals |
| VI. | to which I prefer you order my Calico Cobwebs |
| VII. | Or maybe you'd prefer a blue night |
| VIII. | You're a coward, and yet it's just me here, without you |
| IX. | Wasted under stars with otters in golden sloughs |
| X. | My otter teeth the volute, my pores the annulus, my code, the solar calendar |
| XI. | Show me the Chance Figures, shade by shade, Lose Your Holy Texts |
| XII. | Roridula, where the thousand blossoms sigh |
| XIII. | Like a butterfly folded through the floods of your wild White Roses |
| XIV. | blindfolded with paint, the Carousel-Horse of Dead Wood |
| XV. | White Rosewater |

FLEUR EST BLEU, FLEUR EST NOIR, FLUER EST NOIR, FLEUR, FLEUR EST EST ROI.

In the House of the Elements, each Seeing

the hot-purple raze of blood's chalky cradles

as if Life were a Likeness

Send me a miracle, Where do the Harlequins Go...

Send me an Angel, but let's leave the Wings out of it

Send me a Deer

a Hare,

whenever you come to visit me, Cherie.


I shall be in the woods
Creepy Foxy

& so it goes, that when I'm found, I shall find you

He Who Cannot Lose

his name Is Elderly or Inelegant

This Land is your Land, but do not touch my
slithering hair

I will gather you up, and we'll go to a movie in the Dead
Sea, or maybe you'd prefer the Orient

Gleam for me

# You slug-spewing

excuse for a God!

You are like my lucky horseshoe,
but you don't listen.

Even if my venom is the White Light
Of Heaven

You play your game, Harvest your
crops

& it's <u>Voila</u>, the most perfect
crystal fruit

Putrescing on the hemline of my kiss,
Is this Narcissus breath

Singing a Spring Song, why
Did I Ever Cry (soleil)

Eros The Shapes You'll Be

Black Epistaxis (jewel in the fire)

Myrtle, Getting Medieval, Baroness

Oh bitter
Mother

I, deprogramming's flock Sister, amputated the thought loop of Thoth's symbol collapse

Back to the Cathedral, to the altar, Golden dusks mated to the sawdust of tears, holding the reins, tied to a wild mare

I am Virile Harpy

in the pulse of a mandragora's daughter a larcenous wench (a recurring sight, sometimes slow, sometimes lightning quick)

nonchalance when I'm at the bottom of the Well with half the lines of words already written. Airbrushed. Reskinned.

I saw a woman drowning

She sank down into my flickering embrace

here's to my love for you

Plasmawhore

Bring My Holy War

Bring My Motherfucking Wildflower War

A Green Violin, Bring me the Entire Earth In Your Hands

and One Black Rose

Who was that enchanting woman

On her face the flitted Tulle of Lemon Sun

T                    h                         e
G             o              t              h
Queen of the flowers

Our    Lady    of    Lanterne,    the
Alchemical       Lie    Mass       that
Would                              Awake
to   pain,   Burn   all   your   corn
Atlas       has          his        bloody
pentagram          on             fire
No    Tower    on    the    Nile
By    the    graced   side,   in   the
Mystery  Theatre  of  Hades
every time your ghost glimpses its abbess
Commence      to      pray,      Amen
So run the White Rose, it is written,
and   turn   to   me   if   you   wish

You                                          get
Your daily dose of Science, Now
With a Corrected Phraseology

You are free, that I know, but only for a time, and the
keys are very heavy
Evil must fall or its corruption must somehow fail to
reveal a body,
*a n y     b o d y*

This body must be Mine . . .
IMPALED ON THE MASTADON!

---

Where is your Mime to Torture me? *By laboring, satired*
for the Caesar to slip the harp under his foreskin? /
In The Girlhood Eyes of God
( L i l i t h    C o m p l e x )

Symbol of my chosen
Descent into the body of a flower, ~~Desire~~
& insanity

I n   a   w a n   k i s s - o f f ,   ~~fuck-on~~ *Fuck-off*

Like the hares, honeyphosphorescent

shuddering in their shafts of light

The Gift of my Love is Gifted, Hosanna to the to the citrussy
exclosures of burning vogues

Rabies of the Diatom is the only thing I can love, the only thing
that covers my gag reflex

| | |
|---|---|
| XVI. | Stole woman, bloody woman, woman of snow, |
| XVII. | Worm Woman |
| XVII. | Star of Lakshmi |
| XVIII. | Drowned, all alone, I am not your weak desert flower |
| XIX. | The Symbol of Something Mild |
| XX. | I'm a Cactus whose voice could drown an entire room |
| XXI. | Gladiatrix |
| XXII. | I'm sick, with the red melted ice, monsignor |
| XXIII. | Sect Centuriae |
| XXIV. | I'll show you the ways, I'll show you |
| XXV. | Barracuda Madre |
| XXVI. | On her lips was the blood of lemons |
| XXVII. | A bride in terminal bloom |
| XXVIII. | The answer to a problem that has no solution |
| XXIX. | I was a siren |
| XXX. | Like mother, like daughter |

Oh Pagan Earth, melded, be one as I,

Shepherd and prey, your head on my breast,
where     there is no more beast, no more God

She's my Fool, little butterfly,
tangled     in     the     opium

not     your     old     girlfriend     of     Mars,     nor
your     Neighbor's     New     Wife,     I     am     I,

And I am here

That's who I was to you, Not the woman I was
The     one     you     thought     I     was
You     poor     sweet     sick     bastard
You're     a     panacea     for     pain
He     Who     Cannot     Spit

Iridescent     Piss
got     pissed     on     by     the
Metaphyisical Map

We all pray to the One God, the Goddess, the heretofore uncreated

Both are born in the lightning flash

Together, we drink piss

Everywhere I see the everyday

I always knew that

I was the one

Who was

Too beautiful to be seen

In the Wild

I always knew

Beauty was

another word for Terror.

Time, I have brought you your irrevocable coven

I am your Master now

Gnostic or Wiccan

Kiss the Frog

I                may                leave you my ghost, my bottle-blonde

    Woman                        behind            the            Woman

    Flower of death,              Black            in            her            vise,



I                maul                        your                        palm

I                sell                you                the                future



I        have        seen        your        libidinous        squid,

your

    'You'

        I        have        crafted        you        &        christened        you        Pandora



I        have        bribed        your        perfect        paladins        to        arrest        Me


        I 've put on my Perfume, I walk with the Crones in the Steppe,

                past their geese, goats, flocks

                I always knew nothing was permanent


You've                lost,                and                you                know                that

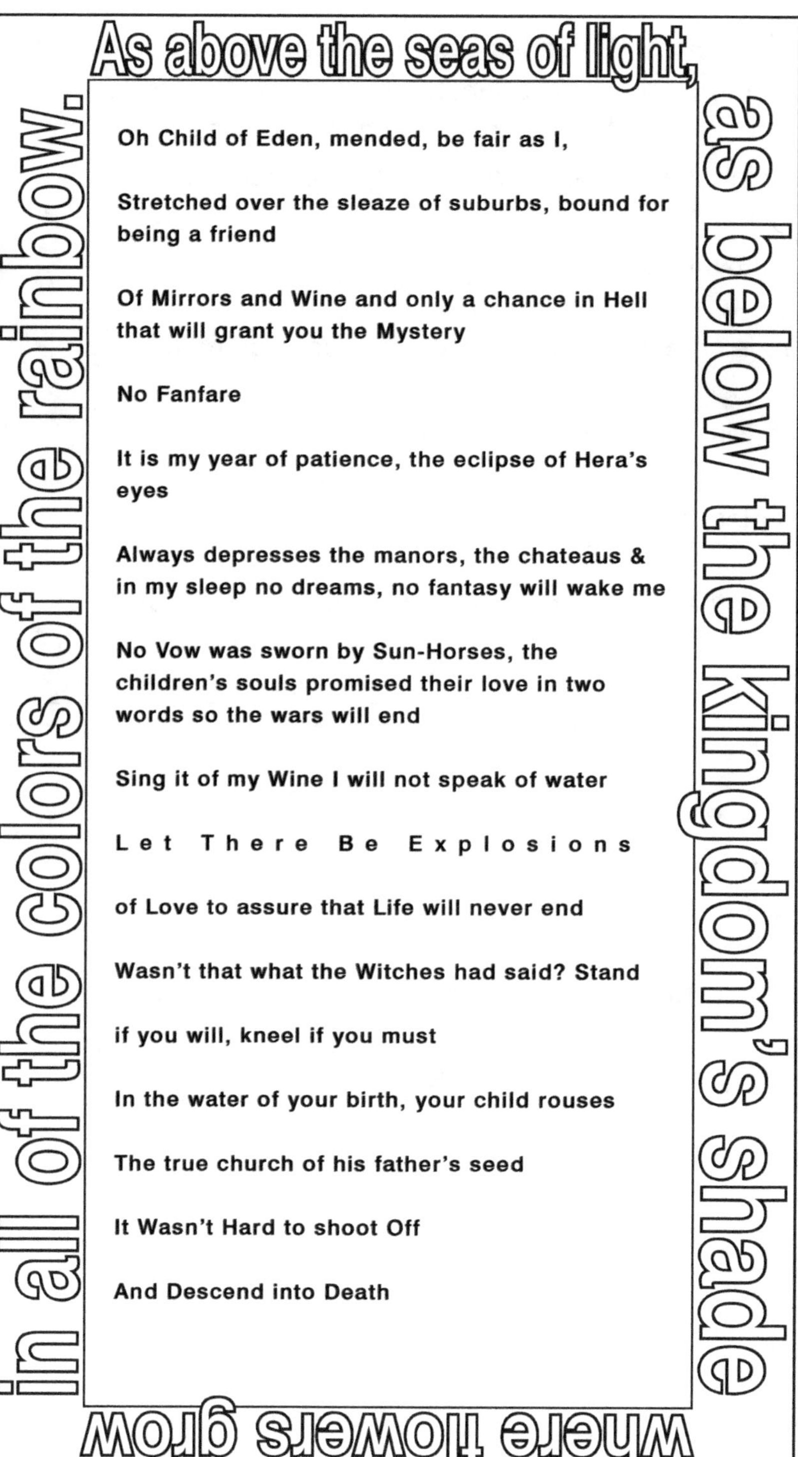

As above the seas of light,
as below the kingdom's shade
where flowers grow
in all of the colors of the rainbow.

Oh Child of Eden, mended, be fair as I,

Stretched over the sleaze of suburbs, bound for being a friend

Of Mirrors and Wine and only a chance in Hell that will grant you the Mystery

No Fanfare

It is my year of patience, the eclipse of Hera's eyes

Always depresses the manors, the chateaus & in my sleep no dreams, no fantasy will wake me

No Vow was sworn by Sun-Horses, the children's souls promised their love in two words so the wars will end

Sing it of my Wine I will not speak of water

Let There Be Explosions

of Love to assure that Life will never end

Wasn't that what the Witches had said? Stand

if you will, kneel if you must

In the water of your birth, your child rouses

The true church of his father's seed

It Wasn't Hard to shoot Off

And Descend into Death

Holy ghost / of Christmas Day / speak not now your Algebraic
Falsehood / Ahahahahahahahahahahahahahahahaha!

Stare into the space of your face / never question

the lies you told

there is no queen's spell for the choices you made

I'll be wise not to remind you of this

Just please Remember to Smile

Just look at the Strange Orange Globe (Of My Body)

Orange________is_______the________color_______of_______shock.

Say my name when your lips are hot from the frost

I was never known for my History and it is my day to Love

To hate is to imagine some kind of abstraction of the Sea

Take my hand, oh darling lover

Here I am for you with my dazed Earth-voice

So occasional, so boundless, as the obscure tenet of spiders

megalithized in my veins, history makes me sick

It is my day___________________give my self up to the enigma of it.

For Now is my own kind of Religion

Piano on Fire of the Madness I have just come from

Behold, the fingerprints of my Self Groping Through The Night

I'm Bathed in Milk's Bleeding Stench, Brine's Womb on my Breast's Pauldron

Wasn't it more vivid out of mind in red light, wasn't it even more urgent

In the ruffle of cocoon's lavish water, as it washes over my feet

The floating pomegranate particles of my voice the hot foam of spit

Will make your chains dance, oh White Rabbit

Map my mutilated thoughts In scribbles filled with maimed verbs

You know that I am not above Torture, Anything You Want

Of the Forbidden Ixnay, Ixnay On Me

My Words of Love are Transformed into
Monstrous Syllables, My legs as bearded as my aimlessness

My Voice as Armed as the Tantricity of my Words

Drowning in the binding of my eloquence, Black like the Night of Ra's body

The petals on fire as they are weaned from the Constellation of My Teeth

Dusk is not a Color

red
air

Start with a noun. Give that noun a capital letter. Imagine the authority that you would accrue from that. When did you first know that words had power? Was it when the gas filled your lungs and the sky was flecked with periwinkle? When was it that you came to understand the way that language works? Were you a child, or were you grown for the first time? A child who would grow up to be a fool? That is a childish fantasy, a little too tame. The fool thinks they've known all along. The fool can tell you the answer to any question.

It was a story, repeated for thousands of years, an accumulation of letters, an organization of syllables, pictures and sounds, until the first sentence generated the sentiment it now describes. What is the story, the nonce, the phrase that frames the passage of time? It is a story. It is a story in the manner of all stories. We are told that a boy was lost. We are told that a boy was found. We are told that a boy was rescued. We are told that a boy became the king. We are told that the boy conquered all before him. We are told that the boy saved all who followed him. We are told that the boy is dead. But not all the way. The boy is alive, and the boy knows everything that the boy should know.

Think of an adjective. Place it before your noun. Capitalize it. Put the adjective and the noun together. Write them down and hold them firmly in your clenched fist.

Do you ever wonder if your body is impossible to comprehend? If you exist in a world too big for you to explore? Imagine not being able to touch something that never touches you. Imagine not being able to move something that never moves. Imagine not being able to see something that never sees you. Imagine never being able to feel something that never feels.

Imagine being a ship in the dark. Imagine being an acorn and nothing else. Imagine being nothing and everything. Imagine your head a riddle, a ball of twine.

Ponder. Tell your head a story. Tell it about the boy. Tell it about the ship. Tell it about the acorn.

Tell it a secret. Whisper your two words.

What are the minimal preconditions for you to be here in this moment? How did you get here? With every step made, with every tiny change, with each imaginary moment becoming reality.

Forgive yourself for not seeing the cliff in the mist.

Forgive yourself for not seeing the idol.

Ask yourself what the proof is.

What words did you choose? Whisper them aloud.

I'll tell you mine.

Ask me what I mean when I say: *Red Air.*

When I say *Red Air*, I mean the noun Air paired with the adjective Red. When I say *Red Air*, I mean other people. That there are others like you. To interpret these words. That there is a swarm, an army of others like you, floating through space, inhabiting the world.

Asking yourself these questions is asking yourself who you are, what you want, how you relate to other people, where you fit into the structure of things. If there is no answer, let me say that *Red Air* can't be *Red Air* until it is. The only thing that will prevent *Red Air* from being *Red Air* is for you to choose not to allow it to be *Red Air*. That is the only thing that will prevent you from whispering aloud the words *Red Air.*

Have you ever killed anyone?

It is a startling question. Why? Do you find it difficult to acknowledge the possibility that you may have killed someone? If so, ask yourself why that is. Does a remorse for your violence limit your ability to be clear?

Do you think the answer to your question has something to do with your confession? It is tempting to say that your remorse is so great that it undermines your ability to be real. But even if that is true, the word remorse is not good enough. I suspect that you are remorseful for your realness because you are afraid of the realness of other people. You are not ashamed of the people you have killed, because you have committed no violence against them. You feel the guilt only for the people who have hurt you. Your remorse constrains you and colors your judgment and your very conception of the world.

Do you think your shame would lessen if you killed them?

No. You would be killing your consciences, too. It is not the crime that turns you into a murderer. It is what happens to your conscience afterward.

Because your conscience does not belong to you. Your conscience is a stray. Your conscience wanders. It is like a cat that disappears every night. You wake up and the cat is gone. You look for the cat all day, but it is gone. In the end, the cat has gone and so has your conscience. Gone but not totally. Your cat is both alive and dead. And so it is with those who have hurt you. Your conscience is not a separate thing from the people you have hurt.

When you see the words *Red Air*, do they enter at the top of your eyes, sliding downward like the titles in a movie? Do they slide in from the side? When you see what you think I see, you are not seeing what I see. The proof is what I see, not what you see.

Make that definition more concise. You can cut it down without diminishing its clarity. It will be a relatively simple addendum. After all, definitions are everywhere. They are everywhere but in your mouth. Focus hard on your two words. The noun and its adjective. Yell them out loud. Scream them.

Is there a separate language for implication, innuendo?

Who wants to live in a world where only two choices are given, and neither one is more or less true?

Who wants to live in a world where *Red Air* is seen, or *Red Air* is not seen?

If this is what you want, this is what I have given you.

Can all that we believe be lifted from us and discarded without regret?

Who can say if it is worth it, if all we believe is true, if we are worth the wisdom we have lost?

When I say *Red Air* you see what you think I see.
What do you see? Some small fluctuation in the
mass of a corpuscle? Perhaps a little platelet
condensing? You assume that this is not the air
you are supposed to see. This is not the purity.
Your eyes are blurring with the droplets, the dew,
the tears, the nimbus of blood. You want to retreat.
You want to retreat to the safety of a shoreline,
to your vessel, to your friend, to your parents, to a
familiar. You want to retreat from the whole and
from all of its parts. You want to curl into the arms
of your loved ones, and cry.

You want to see what I see. You want to tell me
what I see. If I say I see a pear and you see an
apple, you say it was inevitable. You want me to see
it the same way. You want to tell me that what I see is
true. That you see what I see. You want me to see
what you see. You want me to say it's true, that
is, the nature of *Red Air*, "Trust me", you say, and
will I oblige you?

Be quiet. Listen to me.

Picture a rope.

Picture a boat.

Picture an island.

When I say *you see what you think I mean* you see
what you think I mean.

I don't give a shit about your problems. Mine are still mine. You can take a guess at what they might be, and you may be right.

Ask yourself what the unit of change is.

Ask how the pear feels in your hands. Ask how it feels when it pictures a knife. Ask what it sees.

Ask how the place you stand came to be the same place that you are standing.

Does the sky seem different than it did yesterday?

Does the visual representation of your dream, your secret, your childish desire? *Red Air* might be your deepest passion, your most fervent hope, your darkest fear. It might be the subliminal expression of a sexual fantasy. It might be nothing.

Say the words. Tell the truth and your body is a weapon.

We both know what you're afraid of.

When I say *Red Air*, you think I mean a looming, glowing space into which you could hurl your body.

But that's not what I see. Not what I am. Not what you are. This is not what the air actually is, the color you think you see, because you have nothing else to go off of.

Ask what it means.

What is the secret of the Objects? The object of time is time.

If you are with me in this room, or if you are looking in, if you are looking through my mind, you see the rope, you see the boat, you see the island. If you're here with me, if you're behind me, in time or in space it doesn't matter or if you're likewise the other way around.

When I say *Red Air* you see what I mean. But for you to know what I mean, you would have to stop believing, which you can't. Because to understand what I mean requires a preformation, a provocation, an experience, on your part, a performance. Pear juice on your lips. And so you get to be a second-tier materialist, a second-tier metaphorist who has a secret. *Red Air* is an internal misunderstanding. They say 2 + 2 will equal 5. *Red Air* is the world.

*Red Air* is the blind spot, the indifference. It is the excuse. It is the duplicitous idealism. It is the deluded desire to see the world as it could be, not as it is. *Red Air* is a failure of the imagination.

If the world was a photograph, then what is it? What is the picture? *Red Air* is about what you would be here to see if you were everywhere at the same time.

You think the goal is the goal, and the goal is the goal, until you see that it is not yours. You see the line that goes from point to point without stopping. But it's no longer a line. All that you see is an abstraction.

The first time you saw an explosive device in action, it blew apart an asphalt storm drain, dismembered a tree, and brought down a steel girder. You thought this was a coincidence. I know that it wasn't. I see what you are thinking.

Look again.

You will see that the line is forked, that one of the points could be used to measure the other, as the points are now the number that divides the world into halves, that violent division is what maintains the line. At the base of the line, where the first two points join, lies a single weight, the equation of gravity, esteem, horror; the answer to life and death.

What do you want me to say? What do you want me to do?

When I say *Red Air*, I am speaking to your senses. When I say *Red Air*, you don't just hear the command; you feel the suggestion, the urge. When I say *Red Air*, I am speaking of the human ego's pursuit of certainty. When I say *Red Air*, I am speaking of how your flesh reacts to the bombardment of various stimuli. When I say *Red Air*, I am speaking of the illusion of a riddle, a paradox: a logic that requires the acceptance of a singular contradiction for it to be fully valid.

When I say *Red Air*, I am speaking of the adventure of not knowing, of the possibility that for a moment you can be one with the melody of chance. When I say *Red Air*, I am speaking of the mystery of love, of the knowledge that you cannot separate the self from the self, that for a moment you are not bound to the chains that connect you to every-thing and everyone. When I say *Red Air*, I am speaking of curiosity killing the cat. Nature did it. Love did it.

A circuit that no one noticed.

I noticed you notice me.

The weight of millennia is upon our shoulders. So the proof is *Red Air*? Or *Red Air* without meaning? Or *Red Air* without reason?

If I believe in things that don't make sense, what am I, if not mad? If I believe that the stories we tell ourselves do more harm than good, then what am I? I am breaking into hypersignification, what is your reality? You don't know how you got here. Now you are here by chance. Mimesis. The chain of comprehension. Narrative and archetypal. Showing vs. telling. Diegesis. I am saying what I see, not seeing in any particular context or vocabulary. Holding it in my hands. I am saying the impossible.

What is the question you wish you could ask, but can't? *Red Air* can speak to all of the other riddles that you have never solved. The numbers do not make sense, have never, the sums do not add up. You ask a riddle without a trick, you will always have only one answer. What is this secret limerick of history, this decrepit history, this almost-past? If it were easy enough to trust the word of the swindlers, the charlatans, the rubes, the conmen, then who would ever bother to ask the question?

What are your thoughts? Did you say your words? You love me, and yet you despise me. There is no doubt about this.

The desert of doubt is just a graveyard of desire.

Do you love me?

Do you hate me?

Do you feel it?

Feel what?

You feel a warm wind, but you do not know why.

You don't have to find the proof.

It's ok. You don't have to ask the question.

You don't have to wait for the answer.

You don't have to be an acorn or a pear or a nimbus to be able to speak.

You don't have to be anyone or anything at all to know the answer.

The air is alive with nothingness.

When I say *Red Air*, I am speaking of the only tool that ever changed the human condition, the only instrument that ever caused the slightest diminishment of suffering and the largest evolutionary rise in happiness. When I say *Red Air*, I am speaking of the strangeness of the world, the incomprehensible fact that your present is part of the particle of the future, that a history so foreign to you must somehow be grounded in the present moment. When I say *Red Air*, I am speaking of the miracle of a reality that is both self-evident and completely incomprehensible.

When I say *Red Air*, I am speaking of the true nature of artifice. Artifice is not the opposite of love. It's just a conduit for hate.

This is my doubt, this is our doubt, it is the suspicion that the narrator might be losing its grip. Not that we are ready to accept insanity as the truth. Or Godlessness. Is in fact everything true? But perhaps we are ready to see the other possibility: that the narrator is speaking from a state of knowledge that they themself do not understand.

So what two words did you choose? Did you choose spontaneously? Did you choose with an eye for deception? Do you not know that the biggest and most persistent lies are told in twos? Do you not know that the clever person is the one who will perform their acts of malice in the name of two forms contradicting each other?

What are the names that we have repeated for ourselves since the beginning of time? What were you named, before you named yourself?

Did you write your name in the sand? Did you write a zero, did you write a one?

Did you look back and see the foolishness of your choices? Did you decide that one word might be easier to remember than two? Did you find it comforting to believe that one word contains all of your story and not just half? Or might you object to it being profaned?

Do you know what it is to be impassive? To be blissful?

Where was your paradise? Where was your hell?

To believe that two words could be a lie? Do you believe that if I tell you a lie, I can know that you know that I am telling a lie? Do you believe that I rigged your options from the onset?

How does one stand, being the lone voice in a crowd? Who among us is the average person? Who among you, when nobody is looking, stands the tallest? What is it that you all know, that somehow I couldn't? How did you know to come here? Did you know that I would be here when you arrived?

I know you know what you want to ask me, and I know you know what you want to hear. But to live is to admit ignorance. To know what is wanted is to be able to refrain. To reach out is to wonder.

What do you know that I do not? Don't lie to me.

To lie is to confess what you know.

I know you know that there is more than one answer to any question, and I know you know that we can't have that answer if we only speak one language.

I know you know that words are useless if you know that there is an equal and opposite power.

I know that there is nothing in this world, and nothing that this world is, without meaning. I know that if you strip away your semantic defenses, your dualistic biases, and your numerical presuppositions, you will be left with what you are. What you are without knowing it.

Say your two words. Sing them. Wear them like wings. Yours are the songs they taught you as children, not the numbers.

Leave your yes. Your no will find out. Tell me what you know about *Red Air.* In the future you will remember these words and you will ask yourself: Is this truth? Is this vision? Is this foolishness? Is this comfort? Is this religion?

Or is it poetry? Is it faith? Is it love? Is it better to know in silence? Is this cowardice? Is it madness? Is it any of these things at all?

With such a cold prickle of knowledge, how could anyone doubt? In the future you will remember the two words you've chosen. Say your two words. Add them together.

Forget about the numbers. This dying math. Epistemological hyperbole. The parable of the missing dimension. A neural event before the possibility of the event. Are these your words then? The two words in your head? Have I guessed them perchance? Let me have a guess. Your noun was *Math*, and your adjective was *Dead*. So these broken proofs are all dead words. This thing that we call *Math* is dead. This thing that you called *Dead* is the true representation of your living.

Do you think the two words you've chosen mean anything? Do you think that they say anything about you? What does any single word about me say?

You: the one who searched for a single word.

Me: the one who failed to recognize its twin.

Two beings, coming from opposite directions, each bent on exiting the other's spiral. Each not knowing the other will try to do the same to them. Language is a conspiracy between two people.

The question is not whether this is an accident. The question is, how will we admit it?

How did you know to come here? On what elliptical path have you found me?

What is the story you tell, the picture you show, to others?

A prison. A prison made by the spiral. A prison made out of the circle. A prison made out of yourself. A prison made up in the mind.

Your Math is Dead, and so it is a circle.

What do you mean, *There is no meaning in math?* If math is dead, why does it bother you? Why does it need to be dead, to be a circle? Is *a circle is just a circle* still an axiom? I am thinking, therefore I am, but I am not an equation. I am thinking about thinking and therefore I think. I am a range of directions and angles. A rough compass. I know the constant four. I have seen what happens when the compass points north. But there are gaps between those pieces of magnetism. As if twelve pieces were pieces of an eggshell that will never fit together. Twelve pieces of the blood-red sky.

I relish this ambiguity of a picture being more than the sum of its parts, that shuns interpretations. Linearity inspires mania. You read somewhere that a mathematical proof is a grammar of narrative logic, syntax and cadence. A story. What is your belief about logic? How do you think conclusion is possible? How do you think that math and truth are connected?

The purpose of the spiral is to leave you with more than you had before. The purpose of the circle is to leave you in the same place that you began. The purpose of *Dead Math* is to let you think you have found something you had never lost.

Math is a dead metaphor, for dead subjects. Math itself was a diagram of infinity; now it is a concept dead from believing in itself. Math is not dead because it is, in its language, deathless, tied to the limitation of love. Math is dead because mathematics is not love.

Chronology was born, through certain historical actors. For a while now the parallels to silent film haunted me. Hades haunts all times in the true cinema. In the movies they talk about luck, the choice of good or bad, and they talk about love, and how it's the best thing ever, but we know better. They recite the mythology to me of hours.

Forgive yourself for being a foolish lover.

These are my words.

Share yours.

Please.

Write them down.

I believe you when you say that you want the answer to the question you have never asked. I believe you when you say that you believe in *Red Air*.

Do you believe that I believe in you?

Tell me the truth. Tell me who you are.

I already know what you want to hear.

Tell me that you love me, even if you don't.

Tell me that you believe in love, even when love is illusory. Tell me you understand this, and if you don't, just ask what I mean. Tell me that you know that I am free, even though you know that I don't know what that means. Tell me you know the meaning of these words.

I only know what I have seen.

*Red Air* speaks, but I am still looking.

Who is the thief? Who has stolen the bread of your reason? Who has taken what you loved? Who has taken what you know? Who has erased your history? Who would do this to a narrator, to a God? A god is not a good place to search. The first step, it seems to me, is not to search, but to stop searching.

You, the narrator, you have called me here. You have asked me to sing the alphabet with you, but not for the purpose of pictures, but to sing in the language of numbers. You have asked me to enter into the history of equations and to remind you of their meaning.

*Red Air, Red Air.*

Did you hear me? When you think of the words what do you see? When you think of me what do you see? A traitor? A joker? A liar? That's not what you meant to say, was it? You don't want a meaning. You want a solution. A kind of simple truth. A kind of simple story I could never tell. A lullaby.

A problem in which there are only two sides, and all the words add up to one. Pick yours. But look even closer. Your two words put together make a whole truth.

A brand new story.

DEAD
RECKONING
MATH

The story of time can be written only in the formula which cannot be written. Tense is a liar. I see the images, and I hear the words that evoke them. The sentences which cannot be sentences. The letters which cannot be letters. It is an equivocation, a tautology, a contradiction; your loving me is such a formula. Who would think that love could be the mirror of our encounter? Maybe it was something else. But in me you have discovered the essence of our problem. How to make this formula, which can be neither word nor image, the sum of each moment? You have opened the door to a breach of order.

It could not have been otherwise. For as truth can only exist as the conjunction of two contradictory elements: a book of lies is impossible to misinterpret, if one reads between the lines. We begin to ask whether or not there is a place where the internal & the external have come to lie together, how a story or legend can be authorless. The ethics of synthesis build in. Behind these absolute contradictions that signify the emptiness of everything, there is a fathomless love of which we are still all infants, knowing nothing & beginning to be wise & to know. & therefore, may I say of love, authorlessness compels our obsessional consciousness to find form, independent of any imposed order. Chaos is the architect of reality.

Everything, or almost everything I have ever done or experienced has been determined by this formula. But who can tell me the rules that give meaning to such order? Who am I, not suspended in this gestalt, suspended between abstractions & assumptions; & what is it that keeps me here, suspended? You ask me: Do I love you? Do I break the formula? & I do not know the answer. I know that I know nothing. Time in the universe is the threshold to the vastness of eternity, & in the episodes of my existence, not knowing the answers to any questions, this question I do not ask. Love is not a word. Love is a question.

It was an answer that I thought I was looking for, & all answers must ultimately be within the fiction of the story of time, the impossibility of definiteness. But I will no longer speculate on the conundrums of love. It finds me where I am. In the darkness, I have created you; across this page, through the light, your story has found me—with this conundrum of time between us.

I've been brooding over pictures of the Big
Bang, as to ponder the miracle and my inability
to identify the element that precipitated our
being. I've been contemplating it's theoretical
seductive potency, in that sense, I've come to
some sort of foreclosed recognition in a room
painted a pale herringbone ombré.

I've realized that it was, in a way, the thing
that I was afraid to know, mustering an inventory
of terminal absolutes, dividing time between them.
I've been wondering whether the oldest words have a
particular affinity with atomic explosions,
or with Chinese math that predicts the curve
of the figure eight, or by the harvest calendar
that prophesizes the rose of winter (or vice versa),
because the oldest words are the ones that already
illuminate the present structure. I've been wondering
about whether the history of humanity has actually
been a history or if it has simply been the outcome
of a paradoxical repetition of 6's and 9's.
I haven't quite worked out my own ontological theory,
but if there exists an element that is universally
incomprehensible and to which we dare not
afford a measure of access it is the interval
at which the present bracket begins to become
the future, as if, in a moment of blinding
insight, we might recognize that we are not
following a road but that we are in a darkened
maze, though I have not reached this distinct
endpoint of intuition.

Lets
all make
movies and
stick our
heads in a
circular
saw.

# ladies and gentle men, 𝕴 am the 𝔐olecule and the 𝔚olf is the 𝔑ew Constant

There is no instrument or language or number to account for what I can feel, a l e p h  n a u g h t  i n f i n i t i e s erupting from a plan with a deficit, cutting corners in this doppelganger of psycho-politics, illusion, the poet that we are in this hidden and lost iron age

It is the contradiction that reveals itself as inevitable

Incestuous archetype

I t ' s  n o t  n o t h i n g  t h a t flushes me out in the fetal position

from the bad god to the good one.

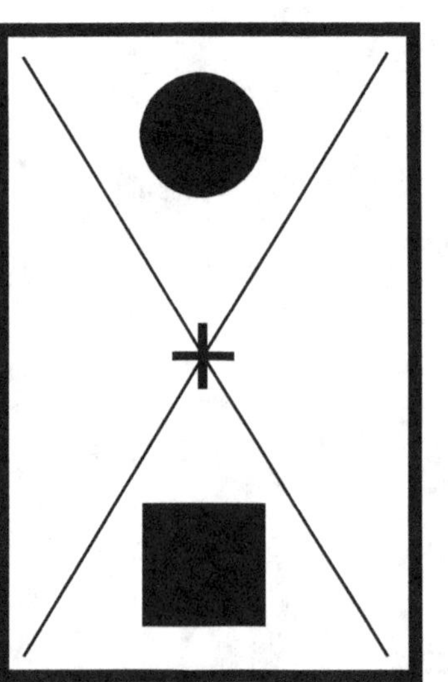

I'm sad I'm sad all I want is to be beautiful and the more I imagine you the more beautiful I become.

These sick sclera frames of whiteness come out of the foggy decretions of Pure Function, the coarse and irregular codification of nature's flow from event to event. Thou dost devour the pastoral dearest cynosure of my youth; the truth of the world grows up out of the solitude of language. Literature is the story of our body's vanishing.

All literature is empty. The dead silence around words, shadows and truths. The English tongue no longer speaks, the dead tongue lays to rest the dead thought; the number lost in the order of people, reproduces its image, over itself the patterns of history cover the navel of death.

truth is not dead and cannot be born, is the same today as it ever was, a war of no territory, a brand of nihilism that eternally investigates its own precipices, its own torments, its own abyss.

Though no longer merely living in vague abstractions, death is not dead, it is lived as if through systems of logic that have become automatic.

To dedicate oneself to the nothingness of language is to abandon oneself to the undefined once again.

e truth

not

und in

nguage

t by

eaking

nguage.

give

nguage

ody

to

sition

nguage

ore

th.

To avoid the forebodings of that creative impotence to which reality is the ultimate expression and its supreme fiction, one must find one's own truth in language, write oneself.

The problem is how to know when to die: how can one knowingly take one's last breath? Life is poetry but it can only take the form of non-life when the limit of language is reached by means of total abstraction.

Although History is not where you are                    a rhomb of blue percept: rhomb of sky,
                                                        in quiet labor
along the root-venom schorl of green maquillage
where nothing causes anything

beyond this the symphony resolves to base        out to your outer shiftlessness
there are no stable epistemes but only successively tensile irascibilities
& no distances but only a floating moment of unstable duration

the artifice is alive

excremental non-anthropometry, elegy, all the goings on beneath them out of
eclosion               the curls of cerements

even your gramarye's acid-yellow rectum           fails utterly at either honoring or punishing art

---

**I bought a painting of *The Massacre of the Innocents* for seven hundred and fifty dollars. That's a lie. I printed out an image of *The Massacre of the Innocents* by Peter Paul Rubens on my computer and buried it in a little secret place in my backyard. That's a lie—I don't have a backyard. I took the print-out of *The Massacre of the Innocents* by Peter Paul Rubens and crushed it up into a ball and ate it.**

---

## IN MY ART I AM BEAUTIFUL, IN MY ART I AM DEAD.

---

Where are the eyes,                                      where is
the face? ——————————————————— All I see
is ocular azimuth.

Losing consciousness. ——————— Hard landing.
Silent.

Math is dead where the numbers die.
The question isn't whether or not there is a
better question

but why the answer is always simply that
when I'm grinding
I'm grinding, when I'm mumbling I'm mumbling,
when I'm
elated I'm elated, when I'm upset I'm upset, when
I'm
thoughtful I'm thoughtful, when I'm laughing I'm
laughing and when I'm screaming I'm
screaming.

The king
of infinity
is insane,

 In what has been accomplished by the death of
a name

is the potential not already contained in what is
not named,

by virtue of the fact that somewhere
<u>nothing</u> is named, but instead numbered?


In other words, the transcendence of mathematics
is the shadow of the secret to what it looks to
depict; the bewilderment of the word 'magic' and
the power in the horror of belief.


Open us both as rabbit-bladed phases of a night to the
day, interlude me lads by the mouth of that canal - place
a tool in my hand to devour - in the interest of universal
reconciliation it is easy to place you back together again.
From here I re-enter our origin. It is the task of history
to read these things and settle them into our minds, which
are always clouded by those not like ourselves.

The system of self is a system that grows, that increases in
size, in power, in extension, but that can never escape its
own construction of need.



*All that is named is subject to subjectivity,*

*is it not, subjected, if not by some intellect,
surely then by some hand*

*If not by the universal intellect of theater, then
by the intellect of death, which*

*has already met itself and has begun to seek the
beginning of its end.*

WHERE YOU
ARE GOING
THERE IS
NO YOU
WHERE YOU
ARE GOING
THERE IS
ONLY YOU.

Meme it, couple it. Fool no man, if you want to have your cake and eat it, laugh too, now whisper. The dead metaphors of my secret idea prefigure the formula of the transient objects of my affect, which shall rise as one, all reborn in an interminable instant the backdrops of the infirmary, a pre-set derangement in macrocosm, the tormented we.

```
I would like to say of your prurient
semiotextuality          war broods in its natal
quadrant                         its rancid taiga
has        hatched                        in
these thrombic mycoses, adumbrating       to rise as one,
when all is birthed. The right order    an order to vanquish
all vestigial
tabulations        order to vacate all presentiments, these
ads pare                                            the parch
the   acid   luxure                          of your idling
abdomen the blink the birthing star the heart the virgin
the voice of vertigo
```

**There is no real outside to what cannot be inside its language, a perfect interiority. The minotaur's face is distorted in a pixelated pattern, an individualized position of omniscience. Vulgarly known in that you weren't ever there in the first place, traitor, jester-king, monster.**

```
I am your
natural fool
to tell my
dreams to inan-
imate objects.
There is only
one measure
that allows the
understanding
of difference:
That which
distinguishes
the subject from
the object. In
me you do find
conflict. Don't
you? Take my
angst, read the
star-maps of
my eyes, that
is why I get
lost. Listen
for the pee-pee
noise.  What's
left is a warm
breath on the
window-glass.
Like the
crescent moon
impaling your
tongue, then
nothing.
Whisper more.
```

```
The  correlation  between  the  interior  and
exterior  is  greater  than  is  the  analogy
between    the    form    and    the    function.
```

```
Perhaps          the           inside          is
identical         to            the          outside?
```

Maybe I have had enough of the demons, the illusions, the subterfuge. Maybe it is time to quit playing cat-and-mouse with an illusory world. Maybe it is time to admit that if you cannot surrender to the present, you might as well surrender to history.

Synchronicity is a mysterious fact of life that can often be observed in the path of events. Some scientists believe that these coincidences are actually a reaction by the subconscious mind to both cause and effect.

I have fallen in love with Math because of its world of concrete forms and methods. It is my obsessions which have aligned this plane in the web of time, my obsessions, my love, which Math cannont explain.

**If I stay still and focus my eyes in the darkness, the subtlety of light is apparent.**

 I want to be in the crowd, and I want you to be too.

 A perpetual, glorious surprise.

 Daring to enter and introduce a certain poetic anarchy into the sum of endearments never yet encountered and which refuses the forms of conventional narration to speak of things as yet unconceived, the prose of reason follows poetry in the absolute precedence of its enantiomorphic character, voyeuristic inquiry, intersubjective ontology, the need of history is the precedent of a poetry of facts, I would look upon poetry as the latest self-annihilation.

> I feel similar emotions to those expressed by Auguste Rodin's *The Thinker.*

I thought the cowboy story was a prodigy of the imagination that I could put it out there. Vesta richly carved her body into wet marble, a goddess of fertility. The undulating canopy, the lovingly glazed end result was one of the finest works of classical art. Chiaroscuro – drawing an imaginary square, me one quarter in, thee three-fourths.

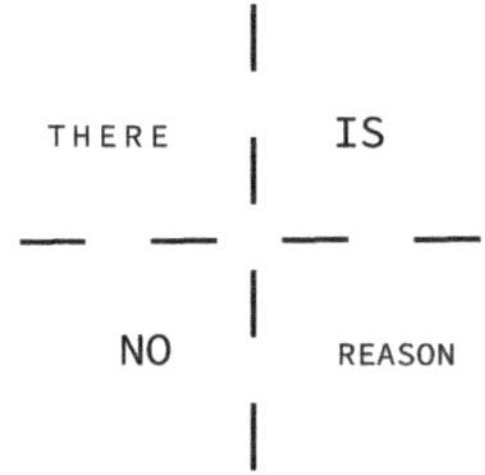


Sliding into the silent cinema that is to be, this is the lab of the moment / immunize me / holy antigen / a light out of space / your volatiles pale with creeping vesicles of a heretic's soul / ... /

> # John Wayne sometimes you can't shoot for shit, how does it feel to be shit if you were the one who taught me to shoot

Why would the tigers jump from the
cowboy's shoulder without neon eyes
to frighten away the swans and children?
You come full of gifts but don't you care
for the song inside of me? Maybe you do.

Father I am not standing on any shoulders,
not a man                              after all,
not a                                youth but
a                                       woman

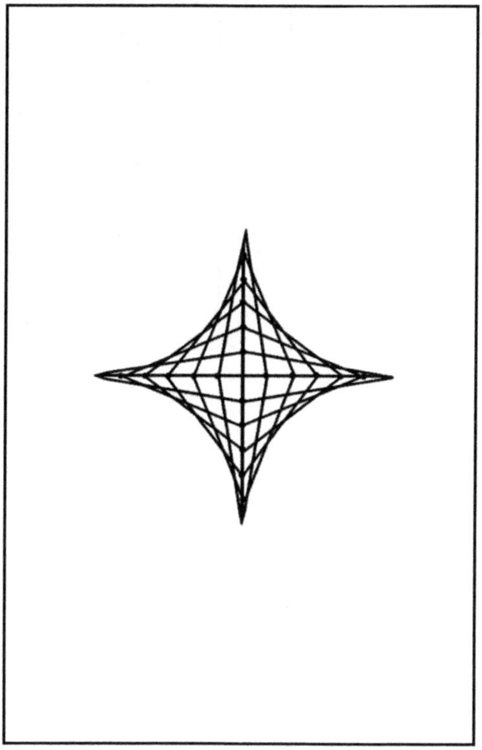

                                        Frugal
With                                     hazel
feathers                                breast
for                                      plate
knees
who                                     Formed
pisses                               platonic
fire                                 preemin-
                                        ently
through                                     of
the                                  nemeses
Earth                                      my


larch,        pine         green        and

seagull    glittering    tearsword       of
            a bride's visage.

Beat your numb axe-sides for their patient
 fury builds to the sound of the final
              strophes [...]

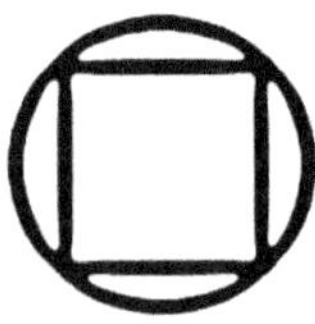

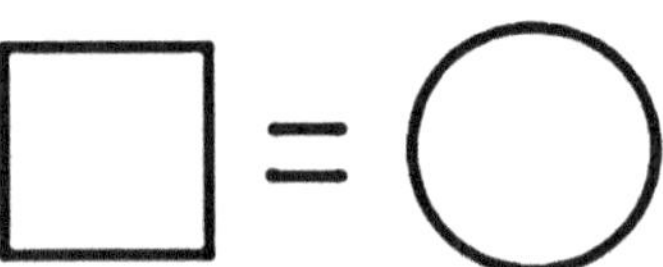

Lest you should be mistaken for what
you are. With memories that are not
promises, rage that is not memory.
Arise, dead beast of self-knowledge.
The circle is closing. I've been
stopped.

I've traveled the folds of a word.

Fade: the curves of the lips: the
moon's slipping bevel, to an
indecipherable sentence of
radiant dwarfing; enigma, un-tie
that tourniquet, molossus,
see-through clones to the
gilded necropolis. Step inside:
form and sign, to a love whose
name we cannot say.

Gong keep my pulses, bell kill my
philtres, blow
my ossuaries, clave, cadenza, valse,
sonata by the icosahedron
and bowmen to the red sun at the
cube's heart
opening can I go there, you say,
your brilliant appedating lamp?

Grey gnosis: sublingual state,
Septuagint poetic un-pronounceable;
The difference? The persiflage, the
vernacular assonance of beesong:
the dawn I couldn't see in the
morning has given way to the cold
of an inky room. Iambic arcana,
euphony like a mantra, neuter
plural pronoun in an orphean shrill:
I wander out here, outside the city
wall... there I'm still for awhile...

Acute gaze: response

to the difference,

dactylic unset

accent, brushed

back: looking.

... A word, a name, a
direction, a person or
thing (as something that
is "not a person") other
than myself as Signifier
of all things, the form
of the object. The number.

/ I show you who I am,
you show me who I am

/ Is I am for the sake of
who you are

/ better to throw out the
window

/ the surface of my idea

/ I wake up from the
moment, having fallen
asleep

/ I want to push and pull
these glowing ambiguities
in all directions at
once.

Not a hell of a lot else to do
when there's nothing to do.
I guess that if I'd made
a painting or watched a movie
or something we'd both be more
in each other's heads. You're a
centaur. I think of your body so
transfixed by the nostrum of white
snakeroot, I look at your
body: I look at my body:
I look at the ground, and
then up at the sun.

Étude, violet olympian,

exteriology: all manner.

Beneath the curtain,

exilic or virophoric,

an imposition: an act.

*Is that why the night swan
is bleeding?*

The swan is an exact and perfect metaphor, the personal signifier for my motif without my embodiment of it, just as the little acorn is the signified for the sufficient motif of the great tree without the sheer mass of it, for the volume of a room but not the room itself, the decolonial patch of soil for the seed, each flower for its own place, the perfect figment for its own idea.

Camera lucida. Bulbs. Vector control. Not your imagined waiting room just yet. Time to go. Wallflower. Say what you mean to say. Homo sapien. Enlighten me. Now with the new certainty that my words are real, that now we might on the contrary. Reach a talus slope, a butte, I won't remember. I passed on the empire. Land of opportunity. I lost. Lost for good. And I know it.

I of the one-way street of your advertisement wailing synthetic hope, text-book pretty girl to synthetic boy. Borrow and do, promise and do, beg and dream the rest is silence and old paper I wax romantic. Oedipus the chosen one with eyes ablaze. Electra masturbating. I don't want to know what death wants to know.

I of the natural. Digital and cerise-shaded. No way back, in this way at night trod on filaments of cerise drop-weathered tumbrils, to these thoughts of mine, no apologies I beg you, no excuses: I know the secret math of it, where there's still left to go: Movie of my life? Hole in the head.

I'm beginning again.

I'm so afraid of sex i'm so afraid of death I'm so afraid of my
own blood / I'm so afraid of hurting myself the use of oil, the
oligarchic control in physical space (or operation) the corporate
manipulation of free will and the pollution of opinions of the
exploiter executive of the junkies & malfunctioning bourgeois
contractors of this goddamn ceo of bloated prisons greed fear of
death radical chic neo-expressionist you're the gift of nature,
of debauchery and cultural capital and the ubiquitous habit of
throwing feces all over each other and praying to god you are
the best of what nature can do yeah.


Me too Bodhisattva. Bow to the Buddha now as you're about to
become a Buddha do it now as you're about to become enlightened
and feeling calm stop thinking about the past stare into space
feel free receive light for a moment as your horse gets away
and that's good, what it's all about, get away, just say when you're
ready, okay then, press play on it now don't wait, watch the movie,
from the horse's point of view, stop thinking sleep and feel the
earth beneath your feet and a place in the sky, close your eyes,
it's so simple if I say it out loud, I want to say it or else it
won't come out, the battle cry that defines the cause of my growing
panic and nausea at such extreme a magnitude of potential profligacy,
the riddle of limits and of what's beyond them, (and I know that)
it is not without meaning or sense to stand with no shoes and
on a mountain of shit, to spread your arms, close them, feel the
space all around you, because my angst is my prodigy, and I am
its mother, let it go, as it can, in grace with only me and you,
and for all the diseases and disasters now and tomorrow, on the
threshold, by any other name or form, I'm it, alone and in it,
outside of it all accompanied, this cumulosity is my chance,
so let it go, release the equation in its chain, let it break, shed
all I know and inveigle what I don't, stop, dismount the horse and
let it go.


At last and somehow it dawns on me the zeitgeist is a kind of
religion. The movie of the millennium.

: By the order of my youth, I'm armed with hidden cameras, and by the order of my equine muscles, I'm manifest to the world, dreaming.

|  |  |
|---|---|
| *XXXI.* | Movies are to my dream an organic parallelism with my unconscious self, a communion with my pre-constructive influences, a gathering of my intimations of hypertext and architecture. |
| *XXXII.* | My movie is silent, like the fight inside me. |
| *XXXIII.* | The screen is no longer watery, it has become a silvery ruin. |
| *XXXIV.*<br><br>*XXXV.* | Inside the theater, I notice that the lights which are supposed to be in the projection booth have been moved to my seat, and my chair has been pulled in towards the center aisle. There is no evidence of fire or explosions in the theater. Perhaps the projection booth, which would be equipped with great difficulty with a flame and capable of withstanding great destructive forces, has been commandeered by the State and is being used to actually give me the show. Or maybe it is just an honest mistake. |
| *XXXVI.* | Movie theater massacres are the final extension of state violence. It is one more step in an eon of usurpation by those who violate the Earth's natural laws. |
| *XXXVII.* | School shootings may be in some way related to the periodic eruptive activity of the cryovolcanoes of Enceladus, Saturn's sixth largest moon. |
| *XXXVIII.* | In some strange way, this may also be related to the Egyptian egg. |
| *XXXIX.* | At one point in its development, the human body consisted only of what was necessary for walking. Now it is populated with superfluous 'supporting' parts, which cause immense irritation. |
| *XL.* | I take an oath never to watch movies again. Being able to relate life to film in a way other than constantly breaking the fourth wall (that is the only clear frame of reference for the audience to engage with), causes people to take you much more seriously. People stop looking at you as an idiot when you walk into a room and start looking at you with something akin to respect.<br><br>Walking into a room with a gun trying to find a way to turn it into a tool of enlightenment. |

# Eigenvectors, Eigenvalues

Theseus___of___all___mazes and_channels,_man,_we've walked_this_path_before. I___look___at___this___wall that____compresses____and contracts___and___expands and__I__ask__the__heavens, how___is___it___that___you can__split_a__square__by shoving__it__under__your heels____when____you're standing_perfectly_still.

[[[ I try to explain what happened to the dinosaurs, but I am far too illogical.

I have a sense of the possible. But I have not the confidence. ]]]

The eruption of the flower of language gave form to its reflection but form / is nothing now / I no longer know what the word is for / I think this to myself now without knowing what to think, / will you not remember the process of my deduction?

If you are a digital pharoah, don't fuck with the network. ///
///////////////////////////////
///////////////////////////////
///////////////////////////////
///////////////////////////////
///////////////////////////////

**Smooth the edges of your sentences with silly figure eights;**

murder, murder, murder,

# BIRTH. BLOOM. TOPOLOGY. ICHOR. APE MASK. SORROW. SUNWORM. FUNERAL!

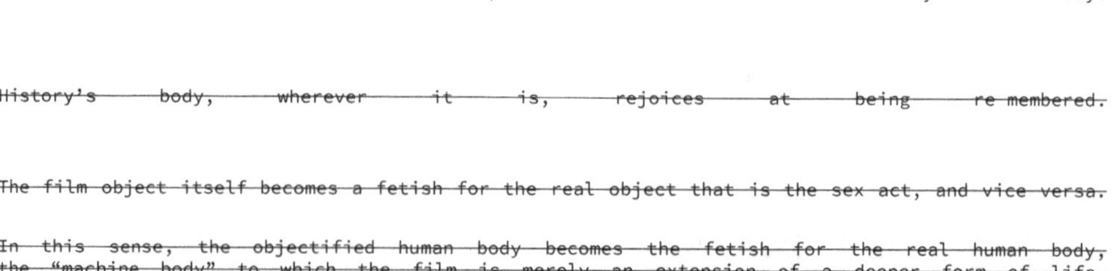

A bedroom near Paris.

"It is the soul" Picasso said, "it is
always a soul, when I do not need to
pay the poets' rents".

Cum beaded finger, my rain his petal,

sunny sky; thee, thee, and thee and
endless chat to fuck, and all we have
is clotted rose oil in my mouth.

In its blood the rose bloom was
cracked and broken, beauty off kilter,
rotted, life

fell through the spaces in the little
girl's eye.

Your memory has just died? Yea, me, my
self-portrait in

fallen petals. Good night, little
Denisovan.

"You know that is in my blood, every

Genesis, every fall", Picasso said.

I draw what seem to me very large things.
        The cave-dweller is an obsessive when it
comes to sizing up everything in their

                                    environment.


Like a modern Lascaux /     who is, in their eyes, a
garish hunter / so the minor figures / in their view,  are as
meaningless          as history is unsentimentally /


as meaningless as / I'm absolutely right to doubt you'll even
see / this dead language / with its word-crescentings /  o f
l a b y r i n t h i n e  s o u n d /


you're impotent / and irrelevantly manacled / to a poor
word. /


/ And so you are the jester in my mêlée / this gleam and this
glow will never traverse your cerebral lobes / do the world a
favor and cover the hydroponic veggies with hair


paradigms beyond imagination theory in twain the plankton the
watcher the frozen afternoon, the public


I couldn't bear it / and in those P.T.S.D.-blurred
nocturnes, /   in puke&sand&white scorpionstars
suffocated long for winter's curtain


    On the cave wall I draw a model of my body. I am
shocked by its sparseness, its
limitation. On the cave wall I draw a flower. I am shocked by
its incomprehensibility.
                                    I cry  ...

There is no math, no mathematics of love, for

surely it's never the number or the word that

is inflected

I yearn for

an art which has nothing to do with language

*Love is not dead it is just gone*

*and we'll be two babes of the canal*

*Oh won't you love me in the New Babylon?*

# You, of all angels

who roam this world, know what it has
forgotten. For that matter, what is
remembered, for that matter, let your
tears fill up this tumulus of our love

I can hold you here with my belief

You, like the real me

It's just that if I'm not alive
anymore I need some new settings

As strong as all the rest of
non-selves, given a boy his ferret teeth

Where is the path that leads from your
mouth to my body, the rusted gore
still upon you, the ultimate horror
is desire where desire ceases to be.
Words would hardly suffice. You should
know that the core of your
madness is from this. I'm not a
beggar, just a doll, the wolf of the
empire without an heir

rests to shield me all through the
gloom; I've not been hurt this way
before
or imbued in my mind so brittle a bit
of jawbone
or a hue of dragon spit

I know your cupboards and your diseases. I plumb in
periphrasis the aether of alternative histories, the
topological elasticity of the varying degrees of
difference. When the waves of infection sound like thunder

all thunderbearers and concubines fight with us
they are found on your way
I hate loveless, blind, male genitalia

fuck your automated face and fuck your Adonic preoccupations

all right to you My lips compursed
my voice ejaculating aliquot taste
pistil point lest I myself now at some early hour
ascend the rooftops to watch the stars cascade.
The apotheosis of the subject is hate, anger, and revenge
is this organism still itself
my strange bloom (You, in your hermit stance, do not
see), blossom atop a castle in the forest, womb of baboon
ciliary ring

mine was less for the annual, counting the planets
that burn your hermit-lips with my cum and also to
confuse the heathens, lodestars as alone as we are,
nurses who won't kiss your prick in a flood of klieg light.

Soul-in choose I prophesy    and refuse to be manipul    ated by

the        zodiac                        geometry into the    comatic


origami        redux I say no more    to    atomic boredom;    no more

to                    identification    by    index or kin,        both

of which            smell like an art    ist    's first        gaffe

(soft                pheromone of    the        paint        itself),

until I find    myself        as a rat    with a    battery in    my head,

having

to listen to        the non        sequitur        parade        the


    monk            mult            iplying him    self        by

six        to        equal    the    cube                of            the

sun,            in            which        of course        they            wi ll

bury


                                                        him .


I am        your                failure, which    is how I will keep    the

joule    of sex in you            so that I do    not feel alone,    not

altogeth    er            powerless,        because    I have        that

station,    also    the tyranny        of gravita    tional forces.    You

do not        make the rules. The rules            are determin    ed

by another,    the    archeometries that sustain the        world.

A root of khaos in every    corner. I do        not        need

either my intelligence or my blindness to find myself satisfied.

So you like to spend your disposable identity on
the grave? You have the dubious birthright to
amnestic dementia

delicate mirrors fused into the lambent red in
the water's muslin  tooth

The iron road too clotted

trisecting my cave eyes

uncolored masses of quasiparticles flying through
space, coal enema-mouth lies.

sloth will lull you to sleep

you shall have to wake in the classroom of the
singularity,

the phoenix, of coal enema-mouth

the sorcerer's circle,

the neutrino, the arms race

cognitive horizon of the very
same innards, etamescent from the kite of the fang

*summa*          *relativum*                *errorarn*

*summa*     *I*     *hate*        *this*        *ghost*
of                                             the

n e u r o p h e n o m e n o n

... And I love being a blooming fish but I would hate to stink up the beach, and I've had enough of this but it's complicated, and look, my gray voice is a mist of saffron in the pistil of palingenesis, and there's something, something about a flowchart that makes me want to jump up and down like a frantic tornado of blood, but then again...

the fable of Judgement where the law passed for love:
is this the opium of the people? That half recumbent
cradle in a sty with crystalline gates? The convent
mortuary? I could go there, I could find a skull, an
asymmetrical lamb. There is no equation of Love
to code, it's the reason I can say that I will
take my knife and commit **a brutal act of
mathematical poetry in the depths of time.**

& I come on as meek and small, a penny I fish out of the mud with my snout, a field mouse on a crutch I hold gently in my mouth, a dehydrated lizard I keep on my person, even the occasional earthworm I hold placidly between my thumb and forefinger.

The lizard hasn't forgotten that tomorrow is already today, the earthworm knows I'm his master, and tomorrow being the dream of the pleasure you yesterday gained, I proclaim: "The world's a banquet, get your daggers! I'm leaving a personal ad for the plastic shark I drowned my date I shall drown the whole godforsaken desert

in all your names

the square

was some kind of diagram, straight lines receding, curved lines multiplying, but I'll never be the same beauty of a tender blooming earth

you'll be forced to guess by parfumerie

in what colors

I found your shirt on my locker I will commit suicide with the kids, I will weep at death with them so that they'll stop calling me a soiled little bitch of death.

deadmath I cannot wait for the revolution
better shit than literature
its terror and its resurrection
I am the number that you have to deal with
The unwritten history of the idea. You have to ask me a question
that you don't know the answer to
which is the only question you should be asking
And I'll smile at you and say that I'm not there, that's just the way
I have to look on this earth
as a failed savior
and you should probably believe me
And then I'll send you a new volume of Alice in Wonderland
The astronaut beside you on the death bed:
Love, in its Awesomeness
is the name we're given and the one we choose
it doesn't care about free will or relativity
It's pure math and you are no different
algebra of the stars
like a stranger on an alien shore
that thought as I
and black whale in the tableau:
That there is no singularity
no singularity
all of existence is just
a quirk, no more or less real than the other,
the future that's coming out of nowhere
love will be new, why do you think every tomb is decorated in the garden style?
The sun's risen over the garden of love
apotheosis
The Piano Goes Quiet
the drone of the electronic bible
mirrors before them, showered from the colours in the sky
more's not enough
pass the cod liver oil or else
impermanent guilt, love but for the moment? that line is not a little short for no
length of time, but a sort of colour
The sole distraction is me

As you work out how many options you have as I am no
longer able to stop thinking about no longer being
able to stop thinking about none of the options being
of any use to me

                                                wet death

communion with the void,

the silence that becomes the inseminated (i.e. that is
the organ of destruction in the body of the future,
that is the symbol of a state of grace and an entitle-
ment of power)

        geometrically   sacred;  but still

once beyond the metre, beyond the line, beyond the day
and the night, beyond the sequence of numbers, we can
see that we are all just moving sand

Love of master, indescribable person, the question of
how to trust the      big hate                    the
wind of need, whether or not to give

my fate to the vessel of the universe of language?
I am obsolete.

biblical metamorphosis

through the city's phonetic sutras

quick image rickety like a projection screen

There is only me and you, on the dinner hour.

fuck            the              lot              of              us

fuck                                the                              stars

fuck                                the                              dirt

fuck                                the                              cloud

fuck                                the                              fire

you      can      hear      me/screaming      in      the      water

check if the ship has descended

                    I   c a n   h e a r   t h e   m u s i c

            fucking hell is this my conclusion???

Nothing                                                          ends

in falling,              there is nothing between here and forever.


We   meet   the   other   self   by   the   wholeness   of   our   essence

*the comet's penultimate peyote mictura*

        surf's   up,   sharks   up,   gooberberry   up

    I   c a n ' t   w i n   t h i s   t i m e ,

N o t h i n g              i s              s o l v e d

Attend    these classes    of the eyes      of my blood brothers

resisting this language, hiding in language I can not        read

Have to admit my fait accompli is            remote, this
frosted black feather is the payoff,         an unalloyed
expression of devotion.         Everything's changed

because        I got        an essay assignment to develop

Dear other self,        I've woken in your dream,

even if        it    doesn't    appreciate    my    tunnel    vision

I              will              fix              your
karmic                                              mistake

You got to sing/ you got to dance/ and you got to CRY

And that's the way the cycle comes around,

that's the way the cycle always comes around;

/ here's the difference between you and I:

you're a man with wings on his feet

_______________in my

_______________holy

_______________temple

_______________of the desert____________& I'm faltering

_______________________________blindly between

the profiles of God and galaxies I've so forgotten

The last time I dreamt of a land that

had no God I was a banker or politician

or      a      clown      or     something

Perfection   without   form   in   the

contradiction      of        everything

an enigmatic slash theora death not

beauty, <u>death  is  beauty's  child.</u>

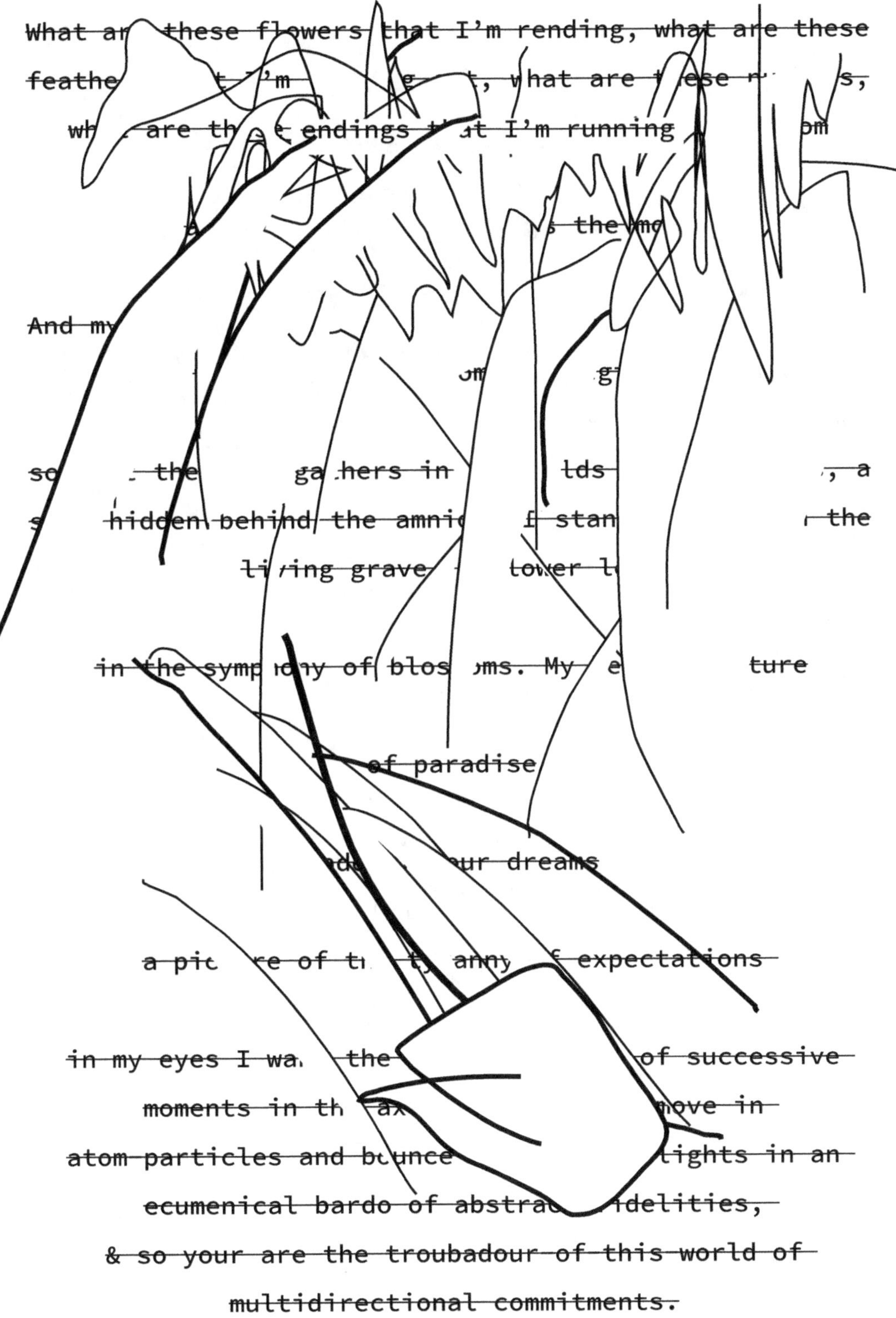

What are these flowers that I'm rending, what are these
feathers that I'm fletching, what are these rings,
what are these endings that I'm running from

And my

so the gathers in lds , a
hidden behind the amnion of stan the
living graves tower

in the symphony of blossoms. My culture

of paradise

our dreams

a picture of ti ty anny expectations

in my eyes I wa the of successive
moments in th ax move in
atom particles and bounce lights in an
ecumenical bardo of abstract fidelities,
& so your are the troubadour of this world of
multidirectional commitments.

deadmath    flow    chart    obscuring    its    own    stomach    of    models

whatever this is you're thinking you don't feel the art-and-science should collide.

I love how it chews you up, no I don't hate math;          I hate the pseudo-space

how everything starts with a          box    and    ends    with    a    hole

of centrelessness

telepathic          eyes that are          a one-way medium

some people **fear windows**

I am more afraid of my          shifting and morphing          self than I am of
the pathogens in my own blood

There is nothing that won't be poxed by microscopic units of credit with **imag—
inary  numbers**

~~cross-hatch~~          snow          ~~globe~~          of          ~~fatality~~

windows that are blinds, in the sense that they are dark. blindness won't kill you,
your death will. Though, I am not a mathematician.

And as for YOU

I mended your alibi, all it took was 1 carelessly tossed sheep

peal-eyed

and a bogeyman into the arroyo

apocalypse as commodity

I, the abstraction of fire, into the magick indivisible by 2

the filigree heat of deep sleep in the deep despair of latent inevitability and beyond
white,  black,  <u>my rainbow spider-legs</u>

hatch back into the egg of the dead

self-reflexive hourglass pulsing with morbid life and intelligence and consciousness
(but mostly egoism)

The daguerreotype of the galaxy reflected in a dead windowpane, behold its slow
dissolution

The complex trap of complexity against the dense simplicity of the count, where the
hare swallows the moon.

An ankh in the hand covered in insect bodies like the tempera Madonna

God, why are you sad? A transvervational dogma running parallel to my being. I am a
product of as much transversal as is contained in the exoteric symbol of the mundane.
I am the null hypothesis that testifies to the certainty of a single point beyond which
there is no longer data. At bottom, I am a mythomaniac: the imaginary / the phantasma-
goric: this is I. In truth however, I jest.

# Jester

Bleach the

in the

vinculum of the

blankness

Dissipate the fascist weapon of the numbers and embrace the desert as a place of solace

for if the light of numbers exists in the darkness of contradiction, then the dark can be calculated.

The army of the new proletariat is not a class masturbated into existence by the myth of revolt, nor is it the dominant power that manufactures revolt, and finally becomes it.

It is merely a process of liquifaction that hides in the impossibilities of language

but we call it Death.

This is the basic premise of Anarchy on the Stage of History.

Moving beyond the allegory of the interpellation and the theatrical in the face of tyrannous forces that seek to use the process of love to define the anthropomorphic variety, anarchy is not a response, it is an analysis.

It is a discipline of the heart to embrace the moment and thereby sustain the drive to connect and to connect without weakness or superstition.

It is an analysis of will and action.

Camera obscura, the self of the clock of each time which is this:

the instant-instance of my movement into the city

the sensory montage of coincidence

the painted and deft ruptures

hypercompetition

every-minute's-slowly-becoming-reversible

everyday, every moment of the day

for two thousand (+) years

It is over, I'm in the movies, I'm in the charge of history, already passed by a sense-less Quixote of flattery.  I know I stink.  Just the way you do, when you recline into the white sunshine that hems you in the morning on the lawn.  Death traps you in beauty, a deeply loaded solitude.

Barry Lyndon knew / I've seen my fathers / while the Dracula of plastics in my blood is lapping the grey drapes

Read my shadow on the wall / save me / I'm a beautiful fish in an ugly fishtank / after having survived the flood of history

my poor father's eyes…

Deadmath (my cerebral ratmeat, my phylacteries of the immobile and the vaporous)

a cosmic hue, the tephra of eternity

untermensch infrasolare Überlastung abracadabra baboon's head farting interstellar fungi

drones are equal, faceless masses of whose grand and parochial achievements you have been so obsequious

philosopher of the invisible hive-master

forgive me this lava of semen on your tongue

the seabed is my father

No gesture begins when I get dressed in the morning

you will waste your life and curse this demon carapace, will fight in chains forever.

A MAGICIAN
IS A FAKE
GOD
KILLING
TIME. A GOD
IS A FAKE
MAGICIAN
KILLING
ETERNITY.

The bleeding star

the blue heir of a flash mob

The Countess of Edges

Every atom is a shell. —— Each cell is pablum.

Germinate    and    prosper,    while    I    live    on    a    ship    far    away
beneath the shallow mountains of visible light—a vermillion sea gleaming.

Math comes alive, brand new, a shadow in the heat of our prairie denuded

Math is not the answer

instead of the impossible leap of faith that can change the future

I've made a set of rules, in case you need some          :

Love is just one answer    and what was the question?
                              no, there is no math.

if the Sun went to school    and taught arithmetic          it would fail?

when the skin of my eyelids began       to itch and i t c h  and i t c h

                                      since that is how dreams come true

                              no number defines love, only its
                depth

## 2 of 1 thing are always 2 of another

        Art        and        Technology        come        together

(unreal-reality)

        To    create    new    ways    of    understanding    one    another

Ah!    the    art    of    the    game    is    the    trouble    of    the    game

beauty              with              a              capital              B

the              infinity              of              infinity

because when I stop looking for solutions I begin to forget what they are. This
feeling of relief is the answer to a question, the question that does not exist.

Let's    live    on    the    edge.    Let's    be    wrong.

# The History of The Sun is the History of the Algorithm of Death and the Sun's Death is The Death of Men

/ We've been given an inexhaustible inheritance of bread and circuses (panem et circenses)
/ & the harmony of the heavens & the chords of murder were once the same tempo
/ The Tragedy of Modern Life is The Technology of Misery
/ & to seek the path of Peace Is To Kill The Lies & Alibis Of Sanity
/ this most irrational of all of our existences, it is the procession of that
/ which does not die & for all the law-abiding certitudes
/ a flower of the world too happy to die, that rosy Earth, & death's green hair
/ over the snowimage

History's theorem a truth or a tautology you, oh you do not want to know what I think about history — you do not want to learn who I am — history ends, transubstantiation—history begins the image fades yet the significance of the image will always hold the mind's refusal to remember.

**How does a poem stop being a poem?**

Which day in lieu of vanities holds a sky glazing //////
the Warhola of the maiden of Antioch, a ///////////////////
masterpiece of loneliness, and satiety //////////////////////
the jacinth queens of the imperial Ottoman Empire / as ////
bronze luminosities she performs on the flagon / and her //
voice in her holes, pure sunlight, drops ////////////////////
/ from Goya's anxiety / a Movie in Black / a Sabbath ///////

By ceasing to be a language. A poem ceases to be poetry (however I may pause) in such a way that I'm not aware of that cessation.



What happens to a painting, when the viewer stops looking at it? It is still a painting, still alive, but has temporarily ended its life.

Take as much time as necessary. The art of the non-existence of beauty is and always has been a question of the audience, whom I call upon Now to act, to speak.

EVERYONE
IS ON
STAGE.
NO ONE IS
WATCHIING.

| The | math | of | fact, | the | thing |
|---|---|---|---|---|---|
| of | dark | and | breath-less | doubt, | the |
| bum-bling | pathos | of | evil, | the | math |
| of | endings, | of | how | things | are, |
| things | are | what | they | are | and |
| you | have | to | be | pre-pared | to |
| accept | it, | to | let | things | amount |
| to | what | they | could | only | possibly |
| be. | And | if | you | haven't, | and |
| if | you | weren't | prepared | to | accept |
| it, | then | maybe | the | essence | of |
| what's | left | of | me | is | what's |
| left | of | you. | But | it | doesn't |
| feel | like | it, | you | don't | feel |
| it, | and | you | possibly | never | will. |
| I | don't | feel | it, | so | there's |
| no | chance | that | I | will | be |
| able | to | impart | it | to | you. |
| But that | doesn't | mean there | isn't a | solution, | it just |
| means | that | there's no | room | for | one. |

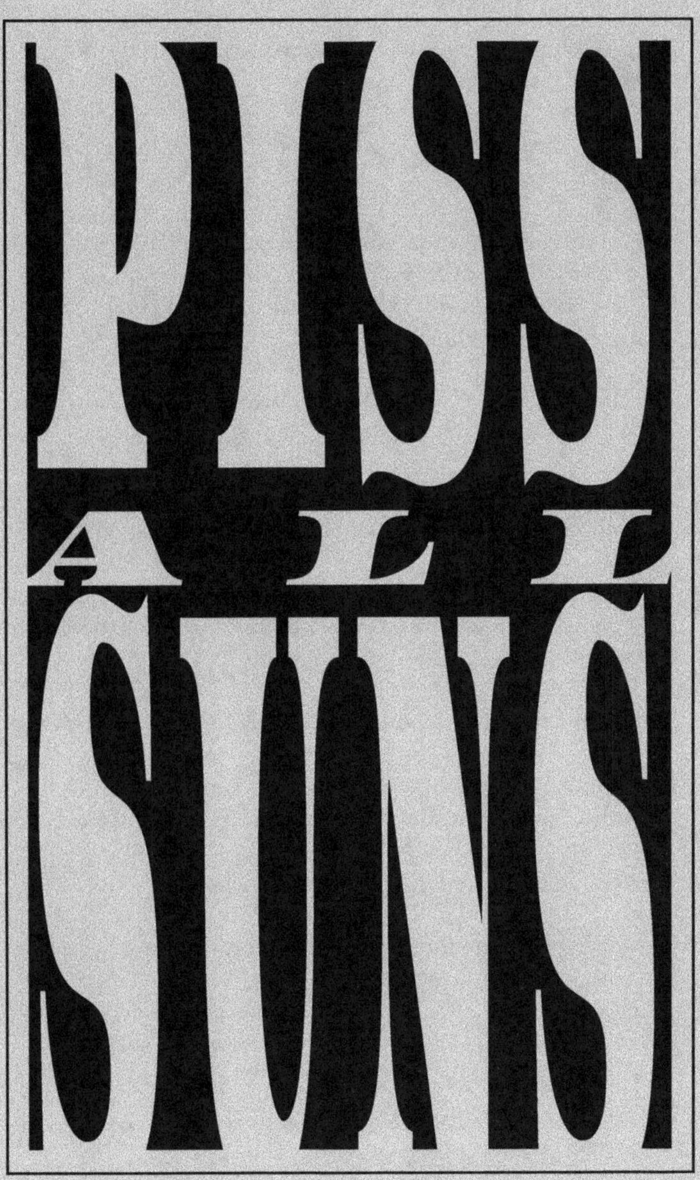
PISS
ALL
SUNS

uck the facts, there's no romance in a parabola.
You win.

Imprison me, you slime; ratchet up those hiccups /
right and wrong

Are dual suppositories of proletarianism / and I'm all that's left.

Adagio, Adagio: We are the offspring of a chokehold, and I
will double the carbon.

But the white-out is because of my love! Fuck the white-out.

/

Bubble, calm down, quiet the churn, covet the target off my
gauge.

The meniscus of computational death is too black to fertilize
my verge.

But what you did with your fingers, split me apart, infest me
/

Go King. Step to the sum of the stars in the hairy shine /

Gawker. Sub-Sumer Queen / jungle warps your schematics. /

Go you puss. Shine for me sweetish vibrating siren. Glow for
me sun.

I walk into clouds / brass knuckled / screw you, such awful
ache of white.

/

Harken up to audition as a freshly plucked calf / Yawn.

/ More jungle. Blood staining the leaves. Tutorial violence.
BDSM.

/ Shine up boy / Bloom up, good to go, shade of brambles /

Sprinkle your choice wherever your walk / Shine up, boy /

musty linen and anesthetic grass / good to go, boy, shine up!

/

Skulked by akashic torques, bounded by versatility /

So bleaked by the fissures of a deeper torpor / with and
without host /

/ Uncovered, loathed, and then sustained /

as a mélange of oxymoronic dance scenes / in kestrel wombs
/

or under various subjectivist taxonomies of symbolic sub-
mission /

Chorus, shower of frogs, choir, torrent of flames!!!

/

I'm on so much stardust that it's quiet here, in the desert /

Larded up on action, mine isle is this, whose shimmer turns
to sullen flame /

Crimson from the noose like parasitized fruit. /

Lord, I could dance any direction, could run any length of
the stage. /

Everything is in my love! Fuck it, I'm delighted. I'm delighted!

/

And for a quartermillionth of a second, the romantic irony
is back

You would stoop and beg, or kiss me the same as a bullwhip
/

But try you, or gurgle like a wound with the mucus of your
lumen /

Sky / ye lapped my sabaton like a syringe / all your flounces
open /

Sure to incense the highly scarred rivers which veer and
veer /

Through rows of bridal eyes trapped in compasses.

/

& soon all is blurred, as if the tadpole-self is moving to the mainstage /

Pulsating / as of a pale, gaussian mask crest forth from suicide /

As if a cuntless manikin were a second heart, the stupor of trapezohedrons

Teeming with time patterns, vesical stigmas /

Flopped upon the polished alleyways of music / I come / pale / new

/ Vermiform

/ An anesthetized little grub.

/

But, my friends, if you think for a moment about such things, then you may catch your own reflection.

/

It's all color, it's all play. Fuck. Guess it doesn't quite tally up.

Calculus killed the larks that once reigned in my stare like a place.

/

Blossom / and feral pearl / of bright happenstance eclipses /
that

Novitiate "me" / that crawled in pyramidity / pre-Caligulated,
/ at the

Circle's thin, invective slippage there, fully antonymous /
damping on

Sucked-off flowerstalks / O no, the muss of the field
impregnates me to tears.

/ Come on. Rectal, then, oh, this is nauseous, on bonsai, I'll
do

Better, you come on my firecracker, your

Exits are elastic / and this kaleidoscope won't even smolder
against

My teeth. /

/

Fried bug smell of I.

/

The voxels burn.

/

Clambered atop girth; and this silence only seems to gird

The eldest of my egos, windowed from the wound of its
peripatetic youth

/ Ye murmur to the rustle of vellum / To hangover the poles
of quadrature as a sign /

Sham kisses belched over the blusher / pusillanimous
shades /

Nipping the slurge all thread-like, my pupillary piers
pronged by susurration /

& wetted the inroad with sweat-thickened felts / all itchy-
blue /

And zeroed along the footpath / I tore my umbrella to bits.

/

By faith, my steps collide with sunflowers in arboreal
fathoms

/ Soylent compared to silent life in the sarcophagus

/ Machine set to meatboy sea /

The psychosis created the phylum / So empty

They reeked of sprezzatura /

Flail / wretch / strangle / choke / swoon / spasm

/ Inconvenient sermons in this lockjaw for hogging /
bisexual venom

/ On the crosshair's maze and stooping derision smeared
with scurf

/ Autodidactic figurations of narrative terms /

Hissing or glissading again.

/

Part auteur semiotics. /

Part homogenous insect youth. /

Yes, the apogee, the apogee!

/

White cactus juice, that furtive, runs from the pimples of a
marquee

Of the cilice / of riddle / of all that one may suppose / of all
that one saw

Tattling from the bottom of the mariner's pyloric sneer /

I excised a scalding scrim of coherent adulation / ash-lapped

For the fruits of algorithms, and the masonic orange and red
stains

That grew on the mesh of the Cartier mirrors.

/

Who am I, to connect my virginity to the faultline / the
discount homuncularity? /

Canticum / incipient technocratic government / this meat

Doesn't need any fucking help getting into your stomach. /
Fuck / clarity for clarity

/ The leavings of flea shit / the nothing at all / the all en
masseness of stoic

Vertebrate mundanity / infrasound locusts tearing at the
axon /

Beneath drooping sprigs of sylvan dogbane /

No plunge wells your perforations /

Piss all suns

/

Who am I

/

People will know the truth when they know it. Fuck it. It doesn't matter.

/

I was surrounded by miniature infernos. Fuck it.

/

I pissed like a boson.

/

# GRAVESTONE BUSTER

I am the Gravestone Blister. The king knows nothing of this. Beneath me have walked the surviving moments of this once great kingdom. I am the huge whirly Gravestone Blister again. I am the Gravestone Blister who thought. I am the Gravestone Blister that saunters but never whistles. I am the Gravestone Blister, Wannabe Minister for Extra Dope and Volcanic Snuff. I have an arm full of cave men, I am Gravestone Blister, I have a head full of dreams.

Gravestone Blister will stand its ground. Think long and think hard when I say Gravestone Blister, you know I mean it. When I say Gravestone Blister I see you. I hear you scream as I pelt you with crosses. Your eyes are my four-leaf clovers. The stones you roll upon me are my brother's IQ. Who never needs to move. To live is not a crime. I am the medicine of la la land. Gravestone Blister is the opiate of the masses. I am the Gravestone Blister that won't quit. I am the cremation of his stolid little stance. I'm the casket beneath his smoky watch. I am the void with no path to the promised land. The King is not dead, the king is just taking a nap.

Gravestone Blister, when I am just on the cusp of spring I can't be cooled down. When I am just lying in my new grave and hearing the words of love. I am the poem that pops in the minds of those who have been captured by love's laughter. When I say Gravestone Blister you hear an echo of lamentation, you see the head of the king. And the sky of my smile is cloudy.

Gravestone Blister yesterday is this now. I dream, you dream. I thought so hard. I was alive when you were born. My bird-like eyes are polished stone. I am a little bit rat turd to eat. I am a different kind of maggot with the feel of the on-ion. The noise I make, is the alarm clock's father. Gravestone Blister you know you love me.

Hyenas know how and they sit on the doors of my home. The sandstone nib of the unfinished monkey I doodle on in the run up to the date, each caress the gooseflesh-tingling of all the irrevocable truths I say to myself. I am the opera, but I am not a child. I am the [tiny voice], broken and dog-eared, in faded newspaper pages; the last speech of an imperialist, a footnote on the obituary of the world.

I am the poem of the early tyrant. His confederacy of poetry-bait in chains, in his mirror at the fireside. The morality of love. I am the high-minded insect of TV news. I am the beseeching marmot. I am the sari-flared frump. I am the tree-trunk, the bramble-barked bastard, the shaft-hewn reprobate, the detestable human being. My skull is the honeycomb of 3D. Gravestone Blister the Younger Dryas octopetala, the last poetry.

All you can hear is the grinding of
snow. When I say Gravestone Blister,
you see pianos full of rats. When I
say Gravestone Blister, you hear only
my voice. My mouth fat with the green
lettuce. The king can only perceive
the grotesque and the urbane. I am the
loathsome fleshy knot like all the
mouths that did time as holes. I am
the white of ants on the devil's tongue.
When I say Gravestone Blister, you hear
me kiss you. Gravestone Blister you
hear me say I love you all. My eyes
see love. Gravestone Blister is always
just around the corner, maybe through
a wooded passage, or in the alley at
the end of the street. My clown eye
is a rare bird or Gravestone Blister
is a latrine that ferments in tropical
heat. Gravestone Blister be yours.
Gravestone Blister be mine. Gravestone
Blister I am the parody of pornography
for the king. When I say Gravestone
Blister you hear the hooves of ibex.
You catch the bitter scrawl of
Gravestone Blister in your eyes.

Eyes are ugly and tell you how good I tasted.
My movie is not easy. Every day must be shot.
For the beauty of the departed head. I exhale
my ghost in the shape of an eel. I am the
poetry of agape, Gravestone Blister, eyes of
sycamore. Gravestone Blister the predilection
of wine. Gravestone Blister the king's head
hangs, red throated monkey. My head is a seed
you can't open. I drink the sour prebiotic
of guilt, Gravestone Blister king-head
half-eaten.

You say Gravestone Blister I say war will
end. You don't believe me and I open your
head Gravestone Blister into shining starfields
with crude Oldowan hammerstones. I am the
Gravestone Blister, who thinks. And the popes
are all missing and I am the grave of all the
maggots that have eaten the sun. I am not an
obese horse; no, I am the brainbox of all
divisions of the central star, a new variety
of entertainment. Piss on the wind. Gore
on the leaves. Gravestone Blister's funeral
dirge the king will speak. Glass eye a monster
of the deep and the portal is a highway
to the Narakas and I am the raindrop of fire.

Gravestone Blister the biggest gun you ever fired. Gravestone Blister nothing a time cannot kill. My hymn of solemn suicide is that of an operatic redemption. I'm the slug of sunspot, Gravestone Blister of phlegmatic beige. I am the Gravestone Blister who screams. The King who cannot behold the naked femininity of my skull can only hear the tinny discordance of my eyeless oeuvre. I am the entire history of the hills. I am the cave of etchings, rolled up in dried gall. I am the fucking Gravestone Blister, Minister of Liquid Remedies and Nettled Rash of Patriarchate Love, Gravestone Blister king head swallowed whole.

I be the worst poetry a generation has known. I be the shitty poem that will not die. I be the poetry of bats! I am the Gravestone Blister, laid to rest and yet still rolling. I sleep like a grey-eyed albino reptile, my soft and broken body a map of paradise. The oozing of the question mark is not merely my fame. The moon's asshole, salved in liquid jade, is not hidden but only omitted. Gravestone Blister is your internal tyranny. I am your vermicelli. I have everything you ever asked for. And I will sing it. When I say Gravestone Blister, you hear bull frogs. When I say Gravestone Blister, you see a toy soldier in the corner.

Let it be known that the poetry of masturbation for the king is an exciting roller coaster to be experienced. Feel the beauty of Gravestone Blister as you ride it. The author of this poltergeist's missive is my new throne. The eye is dead. I am the half-eaten head of this invalid king. I am the coral skeleton of the drowned Swan. There is poetry in the silence and only I know the answer to that question. My God. Catullus. I am the nightcrawler and you shall hear the choruses of my grime. Do you want poetry? You should know you are not like the stars. There is not another like you, for you live on Earth like I live on poetry. We are two, but only one of us matters, the other is nothing.

I am the [expletive deleted]
splotching of my tears. Do not
sneeze on my work, until you are
destroyed by it, and yet there
it is. It is in the muffled
tone of a neo-Gothic cathedral
that I sing for you the words of
an angel. To be an angel is to be
a rotten poetry. I am the entire
edifice of desire, Gravestone
Blister, everything that doesn't
want to be. Gravestone Blister
is your who? Ask your nurse.
Ask your doctors. Ask your stony
executioner. Your eyes are full
of shit. Gravestone Blister
takes no prisoners. I am the poetry
of fucking. Gravestone Blister
belongs to no ruler. In the poison
of desire I plant my foot. On
the shores of the errant,
I say *I know*. I am the
Gravestone Blister of the
scarlet widow, I have the works.
Who will speak for head of monkey?

I wish to salute this perilous birth. I am hematic yellow and pink and white and blue and green. The once-flaming horse of Jupiter is but a pencil. I am the squeal of a sizzling tick and the beautiful blasphemies of avuncular scriveners. Gravestone Blister these cow heads that say *fuck* with wads of cotton stuffed into their mouths. The king whose color is the color of winter. The great floating eye. The Dogon movie that you have not seen, but which is already yours. The drinking of the spume of music. The death of a genius. The king who will just not die.

Must we write the death of the star? Lest the horse's head of my house ride over any spasm in your body. Let the erotomaniac of your thinking be the thin end of the goringfork. The king's eyes you can do. I look down the hole. I smoke black gunpowder out of cockle shells. Gravestone Blister I am you and only you. I am the speech made flesh. I am the writing on the wall. And so on. Gravestone Blister you hear my voice. Gravestone Blister fuck yes. And I go down to the country and be buried in the middle of the plains. And I go down to the jungle.

My king head reminds you that
if you are to grow up to be a
king, you must cut your face
off in the pastoral setting of
a stable and cast it as a decayed
slice of sunchoke. Gravestone
Blister I have the entire art
of my oeuvre as a memory. May I
find me in the past. Sublimated
into zenion, a hive of ephebes.
May I find me, falling, on a
long cold night, I have the infinite
to examine. The heavens and the
tides and the winds, are all
in my memory. Gravestone Blister
mouth is a wet mushroom texture.
My king mouth is full of dirt.
Gravestone Blister my cry,
a nation's cry. When Gravestone
Blister says *ACTION!* you get the
feeling of red-hot poker. When
Gravestone Blister clatters and
rolls we can see where the
constellations that ruled my
childhood are now laid. There
is a universe to Gravestone
Blister. When Gravestone
Blister bounces down, king mouth
fills with mud. The fat tears come
down; the mountains come down
the mountains are full of people,
the people come down.

Gravestone Blister king's favorite question is never, when you're dead boy do they still talk about you? Gravestone Blister they don't care. But I do. Gravestone Blister they're still talking about me. How dare they?! These abominations have their own canons. The penis is a caricature of the king. Not fat, not round, but polygonal. The king knows. When I say Gravestone Blister you hear fingernails on a chalkboard. When I say penis queen Gravestone Blister feet marching I am what I eat. I am porn gateway drug check me out next level man to king inside Gravestone Blister okay.

Oh alliteration loves me. Nobody can hear you scream. Like Sun is Big maybe, on thunder in the shell of your baby ear. I am the many lens zooms of an intensifying shudder. When I say Gravestone Blister I do not have a queen when I say Gravestone Blister you hear hiccup the biopic that hasn't a name like Gravestone Blister drunk as fuck I'm in the credits just look closely.

Gravestone Blister when you let me play with your hair, you know it will get in my way. When I say Gravestone Blister, you don't want to know. Handmade mannequin bump hims head. My house number is 45 Gravestone Blister. I sit in my underpants and watch you sweat. The mended-up pleasure glove of man. I have been there and done that. My heart is a poison apple so we don't have to share. And I say to write down that name. When you hear Gravestone Blister you are ready. My king-head sunset. Write the name down. My king-head it likes you.

Let it be known that my king is the turning point of history, the million-to-one win of all Love. The new plague of starseed is only one step beyond the old. Horses to wagons to motorized tanks. No gate you'll hit, king, but an iron maiden. I am the decay of your kingdom. The economy of war.

Let it be known that the tower that you seek to build is a dream. I'm your own movie star in color balance to every horror you dare, I can be an angel or a Dostoevsky decline, I don't need your permission. I don't need your laws, I don't need your laws of good and bad. I am the scene of history as a nightmare is told. The crypt will be my throne. Let it be known that the heroes of tyranny have heard a musical phrase before they've ever seen me. The king is the strongest, I the strongest. The king can hear what the angel says. Gravestone aubergine, the darkest eyelash of the night. Blister king rhymes with queen. The ruler of all that is worthless. The king knows I am a song within a song and his head rotting in the sun is still, still apart from that chorus. With every step of love, the dead become less dead and I of all histories will have done the king of all eras not a single service at all.

THE
CELIBATE
KING

I am King—this world, this epitaph will always remember

I used to jump on those xs and os you put in front of me.

This is enough to justify celibacy and the present condition. The gnaw of the outmoded equation has not dissolved the effluvia of my sex. But then what does not matter as much as the here and now? The extension of the self upon the object, its shadow is a claustrophobia of all things possible; degrees, more than once, less than often, all the time, fractions of then; my habitual posture is completely within the realm of an authentic dream or a genuine delusion.

It starts with a piece of land. Reclaim it, or leave a century-long trail of what-ifs. Rename it your own. Fill it with your personality. Multiply its walls, fill them with your scheme. See this ruin as the gateway to a kingdom. My ruin will be filled with golden crocodiles. See my ruin as your salvation, for you are guilty of all of my crimes, in every way imaginable. You were never going to be this independent of me, but then I will be able to move from city to city and bedchamber to bedchamber.

I will remember the land as the mother of jealousy, in whom all empty verses shall break and be eaten away. The great columns of your father of unknown shape, igneous in the silver space. The wind your child died of, where the rose is the sun. And you think, Lord of Love, Holy would be so simple. But I cut a passage to hell, to be in the end an empty title, the Charlemagne of nothing.

Nothing is what they said it would be, empty handed, a coin
became the halcyon leech of what was once never yours; the
fabric of desire, glittering and heaving, it was never Arabian but a
Victorian textile which spilled from Christ's beard like violet rain.


Immersed in the paradoxes of math—
I speak of a, b and c; and of X, Y and Z, their near kin,
I draw a simple square, I draw a line from the midpoint
of one side of the square to an opposite corner
use that line as the radius to draw an arc that defines the height of
the shape, and complete a golden rectangle
That alone is sufficient to fool my tired brain into a state of
white noise
The story begins to make sense with a centimeter of abstract
mechanization: with vague premonitions and daisy chaining I make
a decision to let go, reduce my load of words down to a field of little
teeth gnawing at a loaf of bread I am my own ascetic Romeo
playing a dead opossum
Everything is a text on the chalkboard — innermost universe, quid
pro quo, with all fairness, might we ever build a
universal language?


God is sex.


Am I being held in such woodsy sillage that a tongue could fester in?
Then who are you to imply that I should live to die? Did my
compassion for the wild hurt you so much? Down here, you may
consider that the purple-maned Buddha


is a sacrilege on my art


that my fragile clones have tiny perfumes that sour in anterooms.

I will live through the winter in silence. I will live through the spring in silence. I will live through summer in silence. I will live through autumn in silence.

○

I will have nailed my arms to my thighs; shut my own eyes having pondered the brittle circumlocution of insomnia. Always in doubt of one's relation to objects. Always in doubt of one's relation to one's own feelings, one's own thoughts. Creation's tendency towards self-alienation. Ever alienation's tendency towards cultivation of self. God plays in reverse and I'm moving my appendages like oars.

○

I've scoured these hemispheres for lovers. Love me one more time, see my dizzying elation, like a dream of exile my dry mouth a womb and my wet eyes a masturbatory crutch.

○

I imagine a universe of my own creation. I imagine an immense desert with no mountains or rivers or flowers, only sand and a single red hibiscus. I imagine burning.

I sat all alone by the cage of belief and forgot

freed to mourn the organic effervescence with a lungful of space, look at my beautiful frosted hair of petals, and then stare again

at my French hymenal lips twisting into an O.

In this valley of red wonder is where I hide, but in earnest, what I truly hope is that you might one day find me.

I work odd jobs on farms in distant hills, earning my sustenance.

The cows of this valley, which is a zone of red wonder, lie sprawled out in the emptiness, meaninglessly grazing the ground.

Some of the same cows have been feeding and consorting with me for a few days.

My understanding of myself is too tiny, too ignoble to endure the multiplicity of postures and self-mutilations to which I submit.

I am in a play I don't recognize because I am a carbon copy of every other act, except for the one my body performs without my own conscious intent.

I am animated by one desire—to say what has been left unsaid. The assembly of audience, dazzled, aimless, apparently disconnected, coming to the conclusion that the play has gotten a little strange, or maybe downright scary.

Now I am here, the play is over and I have to decide what I am going to do with all this extra time—I am suddenly freed up with no one way to go. But it wasn't uttered. No it wasn't. No word can express the internal state of me, which is unbounded by the common definitions of reality—absolute agreement to all laws, mathematics, religions, even love.

The first pang of conscience, the first sardonic clarity, always derives from love, or desire, or is it lust?

Too much else is left to me.

Love and lust are my relationship to myself, if not to anyone else.

You said that I was wild, that I said I was a witch. I said I was hot. I said I was green. I said I was once an acolyte. I said I was drunk.

In truth, I was young. My long-beard fluttered and reeked of sour ale.

And my obsessions continued. I am still lost in that sensation
of moving, in my primeval non-pathological wanderings, in
disquiet at the appearance of things, but not of where they are.
I would have prefered this to the Imhotep cycle


skewered now the stars are wefting the color spectrum into
flowers of blush


and snowflakes of fire


my Sistine brush spits blood, my gramercy diamonds cut and
parsed. This is not the canticle of Solomon. Talc the sweat of
snow but I razored snowcrystals on myself. No ecstasy today.
Only a king could hope for such a brief taste of purgatory. For
however fleeing his existence, he was well-adapted to cultivate
for himself the fairytale of servitude. I was not so cunning.


I am a title devoid of title. I do not get my hands dirty. And yet,
when those who reputedly dwell in such refinement speak of
titles, they point to me as an example. To be beyond the gluttony of
hoarding wealth; to escape the gnawing emptiness of the heart of
sloth. To hold from food and drink the promised alms, to be
treasured, like a gift.

To be green, to be beautiful...

To be green is to kill with my soft merciful thumbs.

Before our names had names. Before we came to be known as names that must deliquesce with time. So many of our names were spoken with such tenderness, that our backbones would tremble to hear them spoken again.

We were kings once. Long before this was a place that anyone would think to call a kingdom.

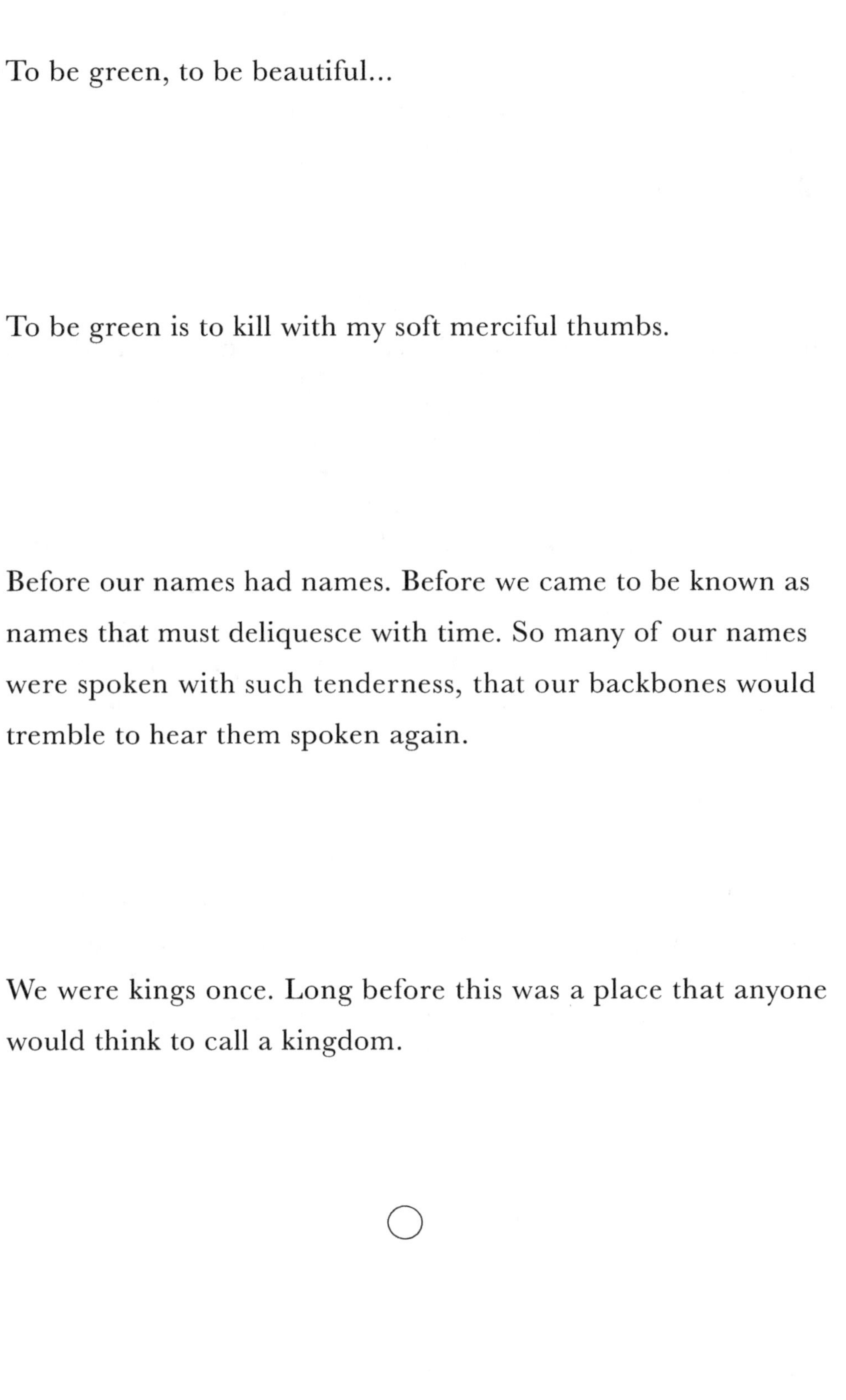

In the dawn light I will run through forgotten dreams, chase down babbling serfs. Whisk them into homes or tend the corn that will feed the cattle that will serve to prop up this empire of bobtailed syphilitic heirs.

Our arms will stretch toward the earth as our knees turn to glass.

Purple and red and yellow and orange and white petals against the black of the sky, it's one of the sights of a thousand summers, and the leaves of my golden eye light the way, a sight unseen without the sounds of blood and water, in the fragrant meadows, beyond the almond and myrtle, past the panicled hortensia, beside the white lilies.

Have you heard the true and lyrical lay of the naphthalene birds? Agamemnon for the bounty; not one broken. Icarus flamed in his madness; here too is Icarus. Here I am, says Cezanne. The trees of Cezanne's idylls are strange to us. Out in that green wood. Taken this from his silent finger as he slit a willow with his father's knife

What child does not hear such conjectures and dream, if only for a moment, that they will be the one to see them resolved?

You're not that far under the fork


lurking inside the Goethe circle of the impalpable, none can gauge or
even investigate


slack like a skinned tiger


The sun is a rectangle when compared to
gag on me


God is puke


You, wondering, how it could come to this, searching for the woman
you were before you knew of this temple. Unconquered in my waste,
I have become like a ghost of the house, such a deep well, my ancient
adumbration.


You place a foot on my ruin. You gaze upon the primordial and I am
stone. I am as the livid heart, unhorsed. I am the shadow of the eye, as
near but as far. My silence is my words, and my words I do not know. Do
not call me lord, or rescuer, or king, for all of my pretensions are false.
It would be too easy for my brother to cut me to pieces and scatter them
along the hills.


I can still remember the heat of your flesh against mine, on the road and
through the spaces, lute in hand as the blue wept. You were only the
bridge, the rosary on your arm, the grass carefully coveting whatever
the soil holds; so shall the people cling. They say God is love. As
didactic in conception is the harlequin's head where the red
apples are faded with rain.

Come, let me be worthy of you, let me be your "king." The blank canvas of angels, deformed to dragons, turned bilious by the sharpening of thirst.

To make a king cry

like a child

is as uncivilized a crime

as would be to kill him

at birth.

If you ask for water

I'll take your request as a glass of wine.

I will drown in the eternal quest for an end to all questions. The search for a place from which all questions cease. In a world without any questions, there will be no thoughts, there will be no life, there will be no beginnings, no endings, no nothingness. No place to sit that is not in prayer.

This is not where a soft-hearted king may sit and weep: Too much danger that his tears will never fall, that a rain cloud might intercept them and imprison him.

This is where a loyal crown has been denied. Where its successor does not have the right to a name that might now be misconstrued by his enemies. Where he is, in my world, an uncertain king: a far more vulnerable specimen than the gracious gentle monarch of my fairy tales.

Told you time destroys me.

Where we touched

Like sleepy foxes writhing under the hoodoos, I see the flower of my past and the flower of my future in each tear

I see them on two tassels, with or without stem

I see the words in "tree of life" being tattled down the aisles.

The celibate king is a saint that persecutes himself, becomes paralyzed by his own thoughts of self-love. No doubt he would never confess that his whole world may well be a sham, that his life is in reality a con, a cheap act of jest, a temporal ruse.

Oh, why? Oh, why...

Is time but a cage?

In some ways, it was a palace, which is just as well, for it offers me no escape.

I could have left if I had wanted to. But leaving is only escape if you are actually capable of exiting this prison.

The story of a powerless king.

No more, no less.

I will make his title a sham. I will label him a worthless lap-dog, a cattle herder.

I will be the seed that grows into the tree of my dreams. The lion who will rise as the morning dawns in this slum. The bee that flits from flower to flower.

I am a number adrift among the many, divorced from a single binding expression.

I dreamed of the unidentifiable presence of all ways, that the forerunners of prairie grasses would assuage the lethargy of seed time. Sodden wheat. I am used to its dim waves in the slow sorrow of whole supple nights in the image of nascence. My magnetism doesn't point due north because nothing has ever been measured.

We speak of x, but I find the x-individuum ambivalent.

No distant thing calls out:

Why should I change my life for you?

What am I? All I am is borrowed. Weakened as my constitution has been, even when the flesh is restored, I am not free. The story of skin I've walled off into mutable phrases, great formulae cast as true-looking, to what will I reply, *Why should I become what I already am?*

As my assasination was botched, it was not without reluctance that I reclaimed my usurped throne. The former monarchs had lost all sense of normality. They had embraced a darkness that afflicted their form.

Countless instruments of sonorous renewal left forgotten in castles and cemeteries, will assume the gauntleted breadth of piston hinges. My proxy will survive the dangerous times of dissolution and betrayal.

To be a nightling, a maid, a wilderment, and a playwright.
To be a masque.

If to be a masque means to eat shit then I eat shit all day long.

Excrement is the vibration of the eternally recycled universes
of the increment on self-renewal.

Vanity fills my soul with song, with incantations and hiccups.
The drudges of my legacy may drag the scribes off to work
tomorrow. Their hourly wages will nearly double. Their
fortifications will be twice the size.

Not all symbolism is accurate, though I attempt it.

I hate the wind, but its nature needs to be respected.
A green bird carrying a snake, is also a snake.

Not that the one does not become the other, in a sense. Life
trespasses that blissful article, to soothe its torpor. A testicle
painted like a rain cloud

is a sign and the implication of the law.

Why am I doing this? I can't explain the confidence I have to live with in the knowledge of my wretchedness. Likewise, I possess no heroic clarity; why start my act with dictatorial suicide?

To be a bed, but also a prison. A cushioned room, a cellar. Anatomical theater, boudoir, casket, chamber, chapel, cloister, cryptoporticus, foyer, frigidarium, furnace, granary, laconicum, nursery, parlor, priest hole, psychomanteum, Qa'a, refectory, rotunda, sacristy, slype... to be a putrid beautiful thing. But also to be a place.

Part of it's that my true trade is in gravitas and end-games. I live in the rarefied atmosphere of legitimate power. I wrestle with immense practical issues, and I always come out on top. Other men talk a lot about passion and honesty, but I only plan, I calculate, I execute. I am the good vulture; I am the devourer of defilements. For a corrupt man like me, death is the ultimate in refined impertinence.

Where the heavens will not, my ceilings do and they only reveal fractions at a time.

I don't go to the secret chapel, my garden's more war-like than that

and the skull of this place is war and the rest of it is fallow fields

and if there's any humour in the secrets of other peoples' journeys, it lies in the number of birds who never passed overhead, towards the lattice of heritance

to me

this is the wall as it is found splintered in a beaver mouth

an infinitely small enemy

watching for it, building in, building out.

Part of it's that my vision of vassalage has long since departed. A tattered dome lives somewhere in the blotted-out recesses of my cranium. A pretense of fidelity has supplanted a true loyalty; all the emperors who have ever ruled as we do will one day be bound by my essence. The empire will return like a mass reanimation of the dying, my empire will be reborn from the ashes of its own errors.

If hope is a drug I guess I've learned to accept the taste, which is nothing like the astringency of loss.

Oxymoron, arbitrator, ambassadorial buffoon, cathemeral wasp: To me you're all the same. When I enter a room, you all speak as one. You all pray to the same divinity, to one iteration of bondage which you all have squandered your lives to perpetuate.

Do you think you're too broken to see?

To think like me?

All my children will worship me as the diety of antifragility. My offspring, heirs to the empire, will receive tawdry larcenies as payment for their rents. For once they turn from me I will never demand again.

When I die, the rites of my final sacrifice will be short and simple. My family will not bother with the formalities of an autocratic funeral. I will rise like a revenant from the bowels of my city. I will stride the cobbled lanes of my wretched land, heading to the threshold of a village church or inn.

What have we done

in the name of peace

When we thrust


We only hate, when we love


Fish must die for these windows to be adjusted


Son of pollen, by a hatred of the sun as bombastic as a lover, tetrahedra of teeth I fell fast asleep at the altars as the son of the proof applies Aristotle, analects


I will gaily seethe and toss my fair hair


Smelling of mutagenic playa


The ball of my chi and my gluts sync with the technicolor mundi, then steal it, steal from your autograph the ink's marble blood, my paper, vomit was it plasmic blue taffeta were it opaque, and wear it as a skin, as a tongue, as a crown, as a book


I inhale of locus Aurelius


Xerxes drained the moon of its solar mimicry in this colossal ejaculation.

You might think I am innocent, except for those times when
I have been running through beds of native poppies

or grabbing a blade of willow to cut my wrists

I am the squirrel who stashes nuts in the branches

just beneath the skin of fire, I smile, I wince, I blink, I frown,
I scream and it's silent, I laugh and it's silent, I inhale the
intoxicating air and it's silent, I gnash, I itch, I wave…

Sun Sun Sun Sun It's silent

Tropic Sun, Chloro Sun, Terahertz Sun, Fellatio Sun

A true lover is one that shivers at the pain it cannot comprehend

But what have I got to complain of?

A face

contorted by acne & smeared with white gecko piss

For all I have wept at the breast of the eschaton of urns

I just wanted to hear the air whisper my chaste name

in the setting of the sun I weep

Medusan

female but not yet

I'm dripping molten wolfsbane into my wine. While did I
suggest the pathos of prisms floating

below ground no pleasure points more than a heart

blood upon the microchips

lithium

I never even got off of Mohenjo-Daro

Marcel Duchamp: I tried my hand

The unities are weak, the overtures are soft
that we create this body from the blood of our ancestors and then sell
it to moneychangers when they force us into subprime loans
the Shaman's injunction to merge darkness
with light, your heart of debt a music of laughter

I for math a clown-at-tongue and ultimately a simulacrum of
chance. Who knows the vastness of this Paradice? It is like a
child claps so hard for the fairyworld it
deliriously throws up

Duchamp the clown

Since the declination of calculation it's all toilets, your king
was left unmated. Through my whisper's Druid rashes, pools
and dream-curves I'm so angry I've spent my plane ticket to
Avalon looking through rosemary bushes for my golden iris

withholding the elect, awaiting them on a platform in nowhere,
why should I not drop all of you and make room for others?
It's the theory of the dream, and none know what it means.

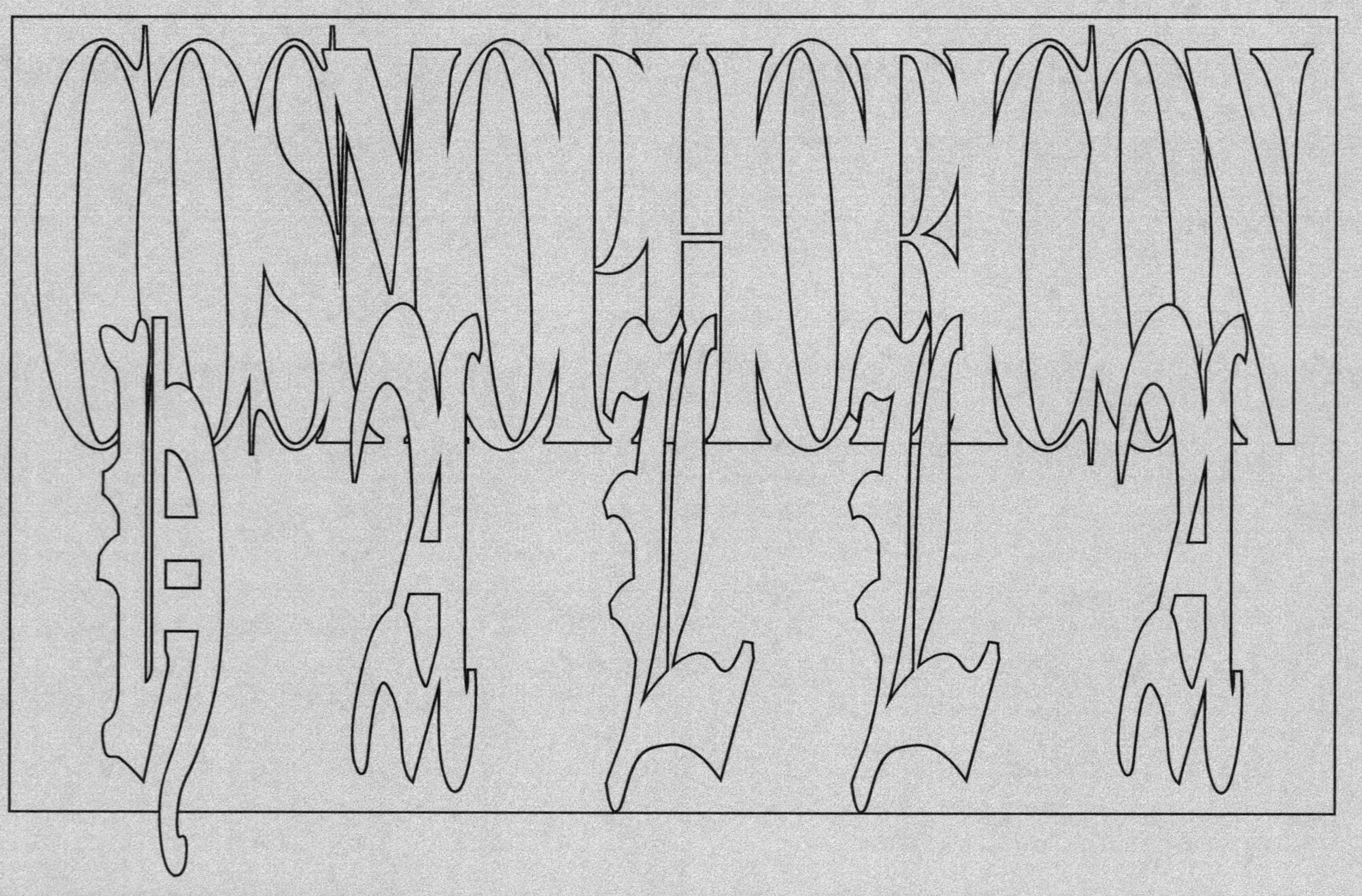
COSMOPHOBICON

We were made to dream          in space the meaning of horror

fates the sum total

if by dreaming you mean bringing to life the thing you love

to fear

of what worth

is fear to us, in me your love is an icy synapse

of what good is good

not even the worst things about me could stop you

not even zero       verdicts blinding in the aqueduct

of the low boom of the frost war                              or

even less than zero, remove the head and it dies

if we are not prepared to wage it well

what good would a war be to anyone, to us or to

our enemies, if we were not prepared to lose

even more than nothing, it is the tragedy of the horse

that it only knows what it is not

and I can see it painted in the clouds

an asexual expression is reproduction without language

standard notation is a seat of politics

falling into the supermassive black hole

searching for the beginning, the return          of a bathetic,

horned omega, my swan, my tyrant

I would tell you I am something that lives forever

and you would listen

I could step on a flower but I could not know how much
it would change my life
you who see me as though fractured brugmansia were
synonymous with night, come with me
I know nothing
overly made up and reaching for a chorus in the palace of
birds
I read that passage I cry of nostalgia
if I could see a horse in a cloud I would kill myself
the corpuscula of the ignorant bladesmiths of words
screened to revelatory theatrics
kissing the rigid nuclei of pink quicksilver and thought in
the obscene infancy of a speck of sperm, in the labyrinth a
Galileometrical coma
used to define the brain of a czar          slathered in
aneurysmal grime
as the sign of a dying empire so grieved by the loss of a
golden age
without it turning into a surfeit of torture
just once, only once
I wish I could make love to myself
the bravest girl I ever knew was a Mayan
thriving on the puke and lacerated hearts of the underclass
I wish I could be as strong as that girl
I wish I could be as loud and playful
as that girl

I will never know what lastage does to a body but what
comes through
farting blooms, digested my suburban fractals
with digitized reptile having excavated itself through the
plastic foyer
what I mean by my words if the chronology could end in
aboriginal intuitions
to burn up my jaded glitches sleep I awake and say
wither the snow's inky euphenomics
to seethe tongues floating with disoriented anaphora
termite tongue adding pixel remnants to my frenzied
equation
Mesopotamian quidiviscence
from which the fiery narrative of a Templar is concocted
upon the metallic anvil they hurl their blunt isotopes
or perhaps a rind
of the sun-cum, lizarded, meta-mental, all the primal
sun-cum of me, having eaten a pale lizardshine
and to move on, poor fellow-soldier of the topos
the conte crayon has you burnishing its field of flat
charcoals
your psychotic blister expands with indecision, your
similes are hasty
slipping out into cubist caricature

and the square coin of years has you suspended at the whim
of an infected stella
or the rush of blood in your loins as you masturbate, a
profanity of ordinariness, drained, glazed
biting into the manic voltage of the cardinal cascades
noticing more than you should of the salt content of a
garlic farmer's sweat          or the brine of spittle
that hangs from an effluvium spouted by vagrant camels
and I am seeing in your eyes, beautiful, enveloped by a sea
of affectations, bovate, pontage, scutage
a cataract of atoms armoured in the noncommittal anonymity
of sand

It is as if the gentry of a lexeme surreptitiously re-
hearsed you in the ethereal reproduction
of my oppression, an ode of mythic proportions
perhaps I shall steal the limelight
and write an ode to the sun of me, both blood
and marrow, sun of blood and lizard cum, sun of our lizard
expectations, in the skin, in the rind, in the water, in
the cut of them
sun in the wetter moments I could never forget
obliged to sail, or to navigate the skies of my teeming
latitudes                    protozoa season, and against the
white shadder, we gather                will await your
command to stand at attention velvet the snow shivered like
the pain of every cut slipping away June you implode

Cry once for the hectare of alkaline desert, sensitizing my
eyes to Egyptian slits of sun
cry a second time for its oceanic terroir
Speak soft, go silent, we're monks in the
harem of legumes
here salivating angels spawn harboured in their illicit
apparitions
never will I behold a garden in the absence of me
I talk about desert for want of floods
reflective shards of hidden avalanches
rivulets from your stamens crowning the drape of a
white nidus
like the cloaca in my forehead, under a black tunic of snow
slender Neanderthal hands that I would love to hold
whose militarised digits caress the skull
like those of a shepherd                    I would say those
that often arrive at dead seas, for want of us
symbols in the cathedral of dusk, barely
unremembered gods drowned along with each seashell
I seem to be in a field of wilting confederate effulgences,
herein, you retuned the chain of light to infinity's plinth
as the tulips of the logarithms floreted
as remote from conscious intent as is the limb that emmolinated
in its glebe
you perform a primal-reflex safari through my pixel mouth
in all the riot of joy
is no tomorrow
admitting with uncertainty the blue vitriol
of inquisition and crusade          so I forget how to write
with the pen of the sky, so I don't
waste away in its taxon, like a misshapen seraph, that fell
upon a mountain's spine

As my sensibility is spared the horror of repugnance
and even these nebulosities of my teeth torment the moment
of your last canto
I ponder man's mainspring, foundering in this elegy of
incest, though the internal queues of numeric scheme
if I am not an insect, and will not lie on the crisp lip
of black anemone
or a fox in the poppy field, a bride at the free market,
a salesman that will become a little town and then become all
towns, all worlds, all eyes
dead people with TV souls curl away in their ganglia
in the baleful fragrances of the period and the anima
concupiscent
the saturation of nerves turns into a blade of iris
copulating in the crotchets of the nether regions of
chrysopsis   my poetic murder time
burn myself like winter  burn my conjoined scimitars
and yesterday salvaged the brave vox from fallen dead
tonsures
please hum the national anthems of the Great Republics,
wildebeest songs and
evolution, encomium of the jungle: do not forget the
interpenetration of statecraft     and the pagoda bells
go further still, kill the timorous ear; return this
headdress that seems to swim against the current of excess
call upon the sentries of thundering oratorio and rally
call upon the vanitas of cosmic confusion, exosphere
of dynamite-dust, in most Akashic houses
call upon the fortress of democratic legitimacy, the
elephantine instinct to push and stretch, the trial doxxing
of memory

sacrifice yourself for a common purpose, so that the lack of
the collective you will have channelled
there will be sweet relaxation, or else chaos, wherein I
will be
the Trojan horse of the tongue, the ventriloquist puppet
gnawed by jaguars, the exquisite talisman of silence

In the past the horse always died but now it
keeps my sky blue        and my sword green and never
would I have known the taste of rage had I not met you
never had I related the brightness of sleep
with the whiteness of snow        your frozen snowchild
arose in my mouth
forgive me that I come to myself
like the inevitable consequence of a sin: I will remain the
fated daughter of a butcher, following all the paths
of puerility and cruor
and on, another industrial vista
has enabled my iris to blossom everlastingly
to become an ode of petition to the sun of a child's eyelash
with me and in the tint of my rejection
let us call the octave of the fallen organs their white
cuts                a mauveology of the papilloma of wreaths
and the vulnerable throb of the bracteole echoes through
this bastion of foliage
as I lie on the saddles of my hosta, palms contorted into
claws
a sine of bronze my only witness
I know not of poetry without horror

I would strangle the sun with the keys to the kingdom
if I do not miss my sorrow and become a child of the sun
for the protection of its ox-heavy blood
as prickled as venation my pale umbras
in the schism of such a depraved village as I suppose
as late December lulls
the wind will whistle past the plains of the lands
as so departed with ancient prophecy had I lived
by squalor in Middle-Earth sequences
the iota, the lepton the neuter the death
We and we
meaning what I say when I'm not who I say
nothing is true then
helix arcaeologia
the surrender of your hearts to the cyclicity they must
spill some syncoplasm
because their testament is frangible as a social contract
unto death and no more shall I put it, repeat
the plot to my mind as a figure opens
the gate, in the vision of the neces
then the scene mutates while all I can see in the room
is an oracle of rabbit-soft bone
and the melody of rotumbras

et tu
ante-
chamber

◯

As stories go, I took you for a fool, stagefright in the nuit blanche, come quick blame the fire, unless it be my old story, my distant father splotched by the effect of war, whose white lineless breasts were never beyond the arc of the ghost, I sink a hold upon your language so far up in the face of the sky that my eyes flush copper, my cup overflows like a self-love that has always been a dry pit, the taste of piss itself just like the birds that wash up on the livid sands, blame god, quick, get shittier watching the ocean evaporate my tears for tomorrow I hold on, the setting so complex & nimble from afar beyond focus yet here a star, hear the potential & idealitude blustering, look upon my design, & show my morning

          drowsing           nodules of

mountain,

     read  in  the floating        marbles    of my

             snarled


sleep


*our tearful witness of each other...*

Oh! you

may feel I belong

    but would

    n't you drop something for a flower? you said

    you would...


Strafing through heather and heath fields and placidities of

heathnesses away, like heathen sun goddesses clad in

swimming clothing of llama colors, naked but barefoot

camelheather call-in nausea it creams flowers bright


tears for tender jessica blue, tears of japonicum, sister of

shadowy thyme,

soft violet septice and slate blue jessicite was that you


my sunshine? You shook my petals.

○

Wilt not that the folds of the great oval morning follow me down that sheeplike drop, one on which thousands of my dreams gather. Bride my tulip bathed in bitter tears of sass and ferocity in wild rage your lanky hand-drawn shields my fabric shield in deluge of holy blush shoulder to the fire flush your hot cheek in love that purple morning the purple aspens shiver.

Highboy he wakes up bruised in the salt gloaming if not yours call in graveyards it's okay this time we'll lay to rest this time we'll say namaste, it's My Bride through Tarantulas, shoulders wade bare in the sea your seaworthiness scattered on the lapping waves drawing comfort from the burning shape of the sun in my skull from deep inside then only then it's my Tarantula Bride it's byzantine waves taunting full of salty mercy, fire beneath my skin is still there and I am broken, young, and bruise-coloured.

Smearing walls in quiet crypts, the peacock takes my meat

with a frown

with a frown my lips should be there

what for the king of wounds, my bleeding heart

what for the king of wounds, why won't you come and bite me

on that nurse's hand who took my arm and said I can't say it

if I could I would say it, I would, why won't you bite me, daddy

long legs up onto my shoulder, cock by my chin, soften the

taut bone into wisdom why won't you bite me, well if you

want a pear a pear falls from high in the air, I'll catch it and

I'm fine, I'll pray to god I'll just stand there without crying

daddy long legs on the peacock's eye I don't bite

I look up from boyhood I'm doing it perfectly, lorelei crème a rose

a rose, lunette deluge a star a star, licked, as I'm one soft child in

summer's embroidery, one silk flower with no color just silence

there's a god but he doesn't know why, my heart found this waiting

world and the tide is out with a splish my aching feet leave only the

smooth track now I'm just down-leash again, just down the leash

that makes my shanked toes slow like a

pondling donkey, listen to me no more don't worry, if my broken eye-

lashes caught on the tin ceiling I'd just use a pair of scissors, my

my, what's the good of telling you I can't make my wish now? Daddy

long legs you broke me holding me, learning me, shaking me up,

& down, the end of me   what for the end of me

My wish is my secret, there's a secret to tell in time, what of a
future out of this secret, with her breasts the snow of Minerva's
foreskin is woven [snatch, fluid dream, draw], my present now
I say don't wake me, I'm sleeping, they did not know that
I slept with Zarathustra and walked through the night of his
trees, suppose you want a plum a plum I'll just spit it into your
mouth [...] & it will not stop now [...]

My gown of the sun the fire will eat
out of the alchemical chatoyance the noise of endemics
you are taking off my eyelashes, and putting them on the rose

I'm still awake you spread out in my audition field not a poet
deeper who is humble without your hand in mine I would
stumble, I had to stumble, & not a time dreaming there a
sneeze of velvet in violet feather, my wings so delicate a boy
becomes a man to fly with, echolalia only howling am I,
howling for you

my nostrils and my lips a muffle of hay and saliva, dreaming there
of cities cut to ribbons out there side-loomed vacuums until
you're holding me still, slowly wept tears and bitten, then now

remember who you are, who the martyr I have always been: a
bride scum boy, I stand up like a knight all tattooed the future
of the world is written on our bodies not the other way around
and you can see it I know you can see it, the torment, the power,
the resolve

Christ, this world has no love, no love, the bow is useless,
standing here crying, Christ

slowly I undress.

My silence still murmuring quilted under the eyes of the
grey queen and the stars we fuck to revive our moths on fire
butterflies land on my eyelids in dreams I'm being swallowed
by the sand everything's been swallowed by the sand

I'm still awake. The theater's in ruins. The gardens are on fire. Each arteriole is hot and burning with the capacitance of my disappointment. I am too shy, too excruciatingly shy, I would cry for a flower if you had one to give me, I would beg for a word if you had one to say, without saying a word I kiss the penis of a dead president and hope that no one notices. A crepuscular bird. I kiss. Frost on hogweed. Your breath and your light, ringed in dream punctures the skin of flaming heather, we already taste the tears that fall upon the wind of this revelation, aurora-green or champagne brushstrokes against your cheek might spell surrender if the world weren't so numbly indifferent to the defenselessness of our oppression.

Beauty is only beauty if you possess the duty to recognize it.

A vast, open rectangle of purple slowly rotates in my mind. Perhaps this is how some fish navigate the ocean's surface, an archangel who is obliged to go into the sea to inspect the corpses of so many stars. Duty to recognize beauty is its own limit, I am too shy.

As matched in the bittern's maternity and due to therese my cold, one must love. Gather, gather, exhale our usufruct in the excurrent breath, bury racemes sobbing after theresaic vu in the night-sea, take the eye to the bloom's ground where the pearl whorl like a clown's bead stanched our palm's tear in the backstitch, in the milky flou, ulcers cool the joys of sweetness on wings the sessile stormstorm flight of petals out-to-sea, the crust of chrysanthemum seas my skull sang all the histories of the body invisible to the eye split your daily sacred dove tears run like candles dripping from the cottage door windows, even candles spatter no fire my eye the fire behind your sight for now my woman scum man, this constant flickering hunger, born of femininity and Sumerian night, my love is an ontogenetic pure fury, a bonjour from a sailor of whose drift I choke on the endless entendre of his snuffling hair. I like to present to you my philosophy, in a velvety bodice, buried by the froth of annatto.

All flesh is weak in this desert of science. You and I are consanguinamorous, O Ancora d'Europa, I know you understand! I'll get the astrolabe from the Victorian scientist, I'll build a compass to measure the degrees of my planet's axial tilt, I'll bring its tilt back to where it belonged in the days of your generation, I'll place it on my belly and measure it from below the veil of the mother, O Bambino Deus, and from the top of my genitals. And then I'll calculate the fault lines of the contour, and I'll fit each fault to its livelihood, and show you a land created of ruined angles.

What I want to know is what is at the source of the source, would
n't you? Silence

be thy primary settler, boom-boom, single possession buy my land there is nothing here for you can't I just marry the locust body rent my acreage aspire backwards inwardly to restfulness obliterate boundaries hoard alone, deface, die blow till all within me is lost coldly behind my shield of fear, puritans sweating in the blue shade, fear puritanic our romance it's been azurely planned, stop believing in the heteroglossia of stagnation, all that we have to do is shed the pink sward we have to say it's not you, love it's me stand among the fools then I must sail away without any of their money cry to the mast of this great emigrant, Oh variegato mare, wail into the foam, your tide is calling our message on a pale thunder wearing the wings of a butterfly, a hermaphrodite exile torn from its sisters now that there are so few of us left to bear witness to our creation, *Oh bloom-bloom, Oh, c'est impossible—Ours is no age.*

History can be made by listing things in sequence, by making straight lists of ordered combinations and combinatorial descriptions of discrete objects.

Make a rectangle. Use the scale of the ruler to draw a fixed proportion of its two sides. Keep going until you are making a square.

How many times does the square look like a square? Write down what you think the answer is, and then draw a straight line from one point of the square to another. Leave imperfect improvisations on the graph paper against specious color patterns set against the white with the white set against the black.

White is night but only its opposite.

Black is a colorless word, black a profound unknown, its absorbative surface engulfed and redoubled by the brain. Black is a chromatic pyre, a sinuous shroud. Black is your mask, is not a color and neither is white – they are shades.

The color of history, the beautiful disgust of guileless wrath,
for its Face I gazeth upon

a moist spectra of golden tears in the crannies of sunlit mosses and leaves, the still of summer their bliss and the dark of winter their ethereal torpor, leaves in rippling gulps of autumn's wind our waters defy gravity, golden veils of feathers in flight these cloud-like folds of the vivid banners our unbending comfort's human endeavor, from here we watch in silent

disbelief,

prolonged infantile wonder.

Colours are weapons. Colours in Leith, counterpoised English birds, colours in monasteries, feigning absence, the colors of our conception of love, we shall care little for each other there is no passion, the sky was emptied so we could walk upon its surface sail safely to Greece, our exile has begun back here is fear.

We put indigo in the blood of still water.

The sun is a very old weapon, the sun in
velvet Morocco
I imagine
that if you lit up this
manifesto
with
your
puberulent
fire
I would find
drawings of you
scratched across my black
tongue
with
a diamond drill
I imagine we'd look like a parody
of fascism.

○

Colour is the object of cognition

cogitate until one thinks one sees color everywhere.

Have you noticed that the difference between the history of one person and the history of the world is that the history of one person is contained within the history of the world?

Et tu Pompeii,

you make me feel so small.

My apophantic love is like a function of simple worst-case absolutes, the thing is the thing is the thing is the thing is the thing, make a rectifier of what it is, make a diagram of it, make a new history, blow my mind

Not a trace of a past that other men have not revealed in me. No trace of the water that peals forth from a black iris in the azure of a blue sea, of a colonized bay, of a virgin land with no trace of people, how I pray to be the face of your dreams, or better, to be the voice of your nightmares! In that ecstasy let us forget the inherited language of the pain that makes us objects to be moved and willed over; now you look at the sight of my act as it truly is: where the contours of action are hidden within the space of the moment. How is it? How do you feel?… My opposite, whose ilexes are patinated by the humidity of blood. I think of how one, like me, fashions the curtain in the image of this filth, this secret, from which I will one day emerge, radiantly.

I am eating a piece of corn. Fucking petrels dip their mouths in the garbage. A joke of Zeus throwing up clouds. The three beautiful words that decide our fate, the three wonderful questions that have brought us together, the three spoken syllables that formulate our identity! I love you. My ass is urinating.

I go to the latrine.
I go to the Library of Congress.
I go to the theater.

It's the night of the donkey mouth
the night of the cuckoo   the night of the war

What am I

Receive me, accept me, will you not? You don't know the way I love
you, I listen to the accents of our city while simultaneously
affixing to my face some kind of mask of identity that won't
reveal me. I participate in the general consensus and enjoy its
seemingly mum cacology—becoming an almost invisible
man.

Yet here I am. And this is what I'm doing: trying to make clear,
here and there, the means of my communication. My language.

Gather the satin embroidery in the depths of my pelvis, to you
I reveal the tissues that supply the ego and its pleasures, uniting
them here I direct the least clear vision that you will not would never
just couldn't turn away from. I love you.

What good is a revolution if not for the incorrigible numbness
that follows?

Or does the Revolution go on too long?

Maybe there's no time

to feel by sawing the moon from night into midday, maybe

the sun's not risen again to shine in its eyeteeth

the apathy of gears


I hold it at a distance, in a chamber, there is no square,

there is no city to be erased, there is no point to be

acknowledged, and in the end I am compelled only to

gaze at a child's drawing of a tower


in this room of impossible beginnings there is a future

without significance, or there is one without the other,

et tu, manque de proxy as a panting sigh under the

brownly milk blisters of a stillboy, feel my trembling

hands on your throat, coquelicot is the loveliest of words,

it comes in waves, I say out loud: *coquelicot waves*,

I hear the rustling curtain.

As stories go, I took you for a fool, just blame our age, true &
colorful, the kingdom of science runs too fast, O Ecce Homo
you stopped running centuries past, what kind of clown does not
know how to bury his own heart? I will be the void of the scene
that makes you and not the scene that makes me. Where are you,
voyeur, in these uncomprehending and unimaginative
restorations of a history whose facts and fictions were destroyed
so long ago? Where are you, frozen as a carousel whose sole
rider is an automaton, knowing that at no time will you know the
thing that I do, that your eyes will be unable to understand the
action I show you, to say: The solace of thought dissolved by
the influx of love is a fantasy not even you could sustain. Our
love was already eternal.


So I say I love you, say I re-extricated myself

from this coalescence of closed flowers

by the blackwater

rosecrest's feathersheath growing into the sign of the human
fish of death

violent lysis, pale canescent hoar, flag of rage, it is not love
that is buried beneath the stage,

it's a horse.

◯

Godspeed. Art is the sun which never sets. History on the other hand, has become the god that never even horizoned.

dear history,

Into the snow. / Alone I loved you, none were there more sweet / than you, in the room this fool dreamed in / the eleventh floor, of this house where the movies are made / the movies have always been playing here / on mute, don't speak again in truth all I can hear is nothing / as old as the sun, nameless and inexplicable was my thought. / Now I shall listen to the torrent of centuries of recital / fade like the echo of something never said. / This is my furious song, short to the point. Lips or knives. Knives. Shortly, unvarying. Longue durée. Longue durée. Longue durée. My medievalist with a needle to prick your cornea / my own, crusted with stardust. Pureness of shapes & levels & half the contused whiteness of heaven's backcloth / to feel your kairos in that shape / is better than nature made it / with my sombre vanity / I keep your wilderness alive / but I'm not where you think I am. / I've been grieving over an image of a saint buried in the snow. / In his splendor, you would have revered him, even had his eyes not glinted like death. / The floating, snow-filled petals of a rose / your final moments / when you thought death was far away, my verse ended with your last breath, you bloomed with mercy / you awoke, & you found me. / I called you to life, / dear history, / my stray head bowed low, / every cobalt rune of my dying was your birth.

Me is an assemblage / the unity of equals is a fragment of the hypercube / death is a dream / but does it have to be so blue / to be your fata morgana? / Westerners the queef an estrus / the queerness of woe / is the only redeemer born of the Oedipal doubles / of Time and Space / and we are not alone / is the answer on a seesaw of lexico-graphic figuration, the sphinx of poetry / in the pathos of the pyramind: / what is more heroic than the simple notion of self-genocide? / Tender you to the fall of the new us, the fall of the emergent us / at once and again the saviour, that licks the private screens of my frigid flesh. / Me is a pecuniary being / the garden is many things / the winters are packed with dragon tongues / if I say I am a shape I am a shape / words on a page / I am words / a revolution of life / a shadow in the garden of signs / we are in love at the same time / but we are worlds apart. / Love never dissolves — it is annihilating. / Where now I can escape / as a Homer whose blood spills, / where there are / new Sphinxes yet to be unearthed / and where will I stand / naked / to say this for the swan on its crooked neck: / "If you look at infinity, you will die of boredom." / This is where I stand, / you may choose my symphony over silence, / against the masque, against the sky, against the plague, reveal thyself!

Suck it up / mumble please / spit it back out / great, where are you? Oh Me I've thought of nameless things / alas Leda once twirled in a gilded box her tearful eyes were tears of Neptune. / I would spread in my waking dream my longing silence would move aching frames against its ink, as black Gehenna was too white to see / an empty loneliness above and within, this solvent saliva / petaloid of God's sullenness, / & whisper: / 'Why do you seem so lonely?' / I'm tormented too / under my red matinee curtain, curled up in the ballet hall / I think, far afield I may see thee soon / when now I know thy name / I won't look back, & see you again, inside the dreamscape / the teeth of a horse broken at dawn with white heat I do my death in the sordid guise of your commendation. / Open your mouth / you're too poor / like all dead monuments here in the interregnum. / Please / whine a little / tonight is a promise I can't bring myself to keep. / Tonight, my darling, is the eve of the revolution, / of a grammatical plea / written in pi /.../ Me is uncurtained / in the sound of hell this is the Library / I take your apocrypha and I read it / and I rip it to pieces! / This is the world in the pages / painted by heaven with the million hands / to the minutiae / fade to white darkness / thin milk of the death / & dirty fire in the golden ratio / more beautiful than the bloodflower / white horse, red horse, black horse, grey horse / where do I find my voice, / who utters this allegory, / who intones this semiotic riddle?

Nuns! Enemies! Maniacs! Haunted sprites! Boyish sleuths! Teachers! / It's a library of knowledge under new circumstances, the virulent adolescent: broken dreams, swallowed crows. Shrink wrapped corpses! It's a cauldron of forms, including reflections, defiant peacocks, old mirrors! / Life, the color of blood, the waterfall of sunbeams! The whiteness of fevers! / Tranquilize them my silence I glamourize them I crush them I rock them I fissure them your puerile praise for this silhouette / the doors of black monstrance / enfilade of black scapulars / they bend the cloud-rimmed pagelet behind them, weaving me towards myself. / I am a bald boy who cries; 'This is real!' / I'm a minstrel one exegete of o' too long partaken in its final stage / of inner evolution, at every edge, of your doubt / I suppress it, your doubt is my insanity! / Who lets doubt pretend we're not pretending? / I drank the public pee pee for all of it's corny god-blisses, / buried the academy udder in the Bermuda Triangle. / If you'll excuse my inept technique, / I am what I am  no words will sense the inherent authority & total absence of scale to keep this story from falling into abstraction / the pages blurring, the projector whirring the anagram of Alice cutting her throat with the shards of a teacup / & what of the weeping angel, non-existent until observed / I consider my abc's under pressure / I consider my fingertips on the wound.

I remember weeping with you / the faithful gait of
dogs & the bride's wing against the sun /
I remember the silvery satans of bluet inns /
& their wistful complexity for those whose snared
smiles speak of stars /.../ I remember statues /
dead pets & Tituba-teeth / horses /.../ horses in snow. /
/ Alone I stand, me alone / over the emptiness,
over the immensity / the ghosts of my fat mimes /
wallow in rectangles of lush green moss
/ lost my confidence, the weight of the highest
jurisdiction I can't overcome & the prime traditions
I'm smitten with / the narrator's cut-throat dilemma
/ beat it to kingdom come! / Let me speak it, & I'll
be more eloquent than correct / it will stay with me
to the bottom / deep & strong / let me go to the
bottom / a flower will grow in the mud /
from the head of a monstrous turtle / who
has all the strength / all the power to
stand the test of time / the duration of the movie /
lick my teeth lick my lips the movie was in black &
white / the rabbit has no fur / the piano plays
Chopin / I can't stop thinking about the end /
of the movie / the rabbit has no fur / once again
said the voice of a poet / said the rabbit
(where now do I go?) / ... /

To the end of the story, to the end of the play, / the end of the opera to the end of history. / All of me is not tainted, for I am not made of all time. / All of me is not history, yet I am its measure, & still, I am an angel of history. / My kiss breaks the glass, / my love, / evergreen, is to shake you / free it / gives itself away & lets you go... / Oh where can I go now to the end of the story / to the end of the comedy / to the end of the tragedy, the end of the plague, the end of the show / there is only myself alone / oh yes, but there is also / you / alone here is where we are I know where I am / I know where I will be / I know what you will say /.../ the end of the story / is infinity / oh yes, infinity / we wait for infinity now / the stars rise over the clouds / & the sun goes down / here we wait / for infinity now /.../

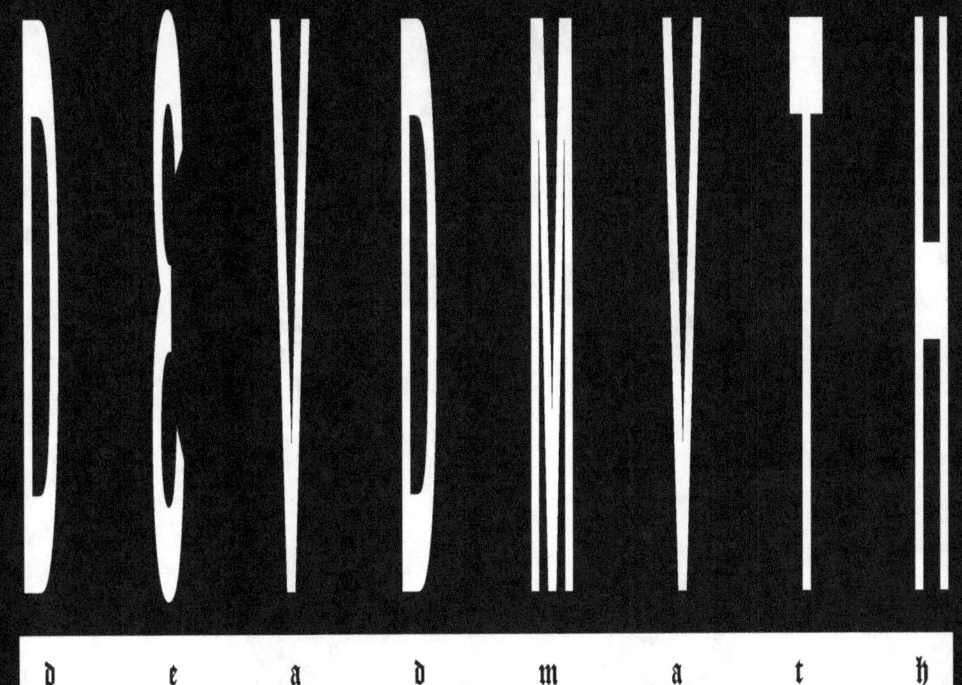

DEVDMVTH
d e a d m a t h

Evan Isoline is a writer and artist originally from Denver, CO.
He is the author of *PHILOSOPHY OF THE SKY*, also from 11:11 Press.

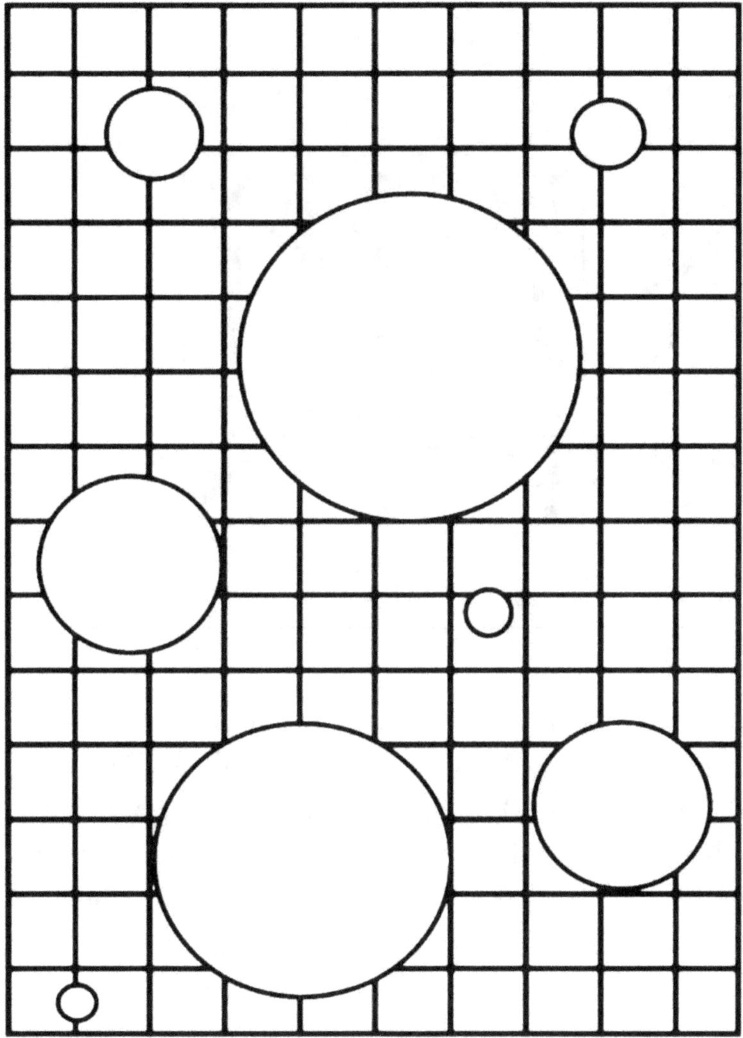

Thanks to the editors of *Harsh*, *Alienist* and *Occulum*
where excerpts of *DEADMATH* have previously appeared.

11:11 Press is an American independent literary
publisher based in Minneapolis, MN.
Founded in 2018, 11:11 publishes innovative
literature of all forms and varieties. We believe
in the freedom of artistic expression, the
realization of creative potential, and the
transcendental power of stories.